MW00422695

HEARTSONG LULLABY

HEARTSONG LULLABY

•

JANE McBRIDE CHOATE

AVALON BOOKS
THOMAS BOUREGY AND COMPANY, INC.
401 LAFAYETTE STREET
NEW YORK, NEW YORK 10003

PRINTED IN THE UNITED STATES OF AMERICA
ON ACID-FREE PAPER
BY HADDON CRAFTSMEN, BLOOMSBURG, PENNSYLVANIA

To The Dinner Club—Janet and Dean, Margie and Jim, Jeannie and Dave, Sandy and Rod, Maggie and Jim, Ivy and Scott, friends who have become family.

Chapter One

Luke MacAllister tipped his chair back and listened to the bickering of the Flintrock school board.

"What we need is an old-fashioned school-marm," eighty-three-year-old Eustace Farley said. "Those were the days. One-room school, one teacher—"

"Sounds like something out of the last century," Norton Hatch, another member of the board, interrupted.

"What's wrong with that?" Eustace demanded, bushy brows drawn together in a fierce scowl. "That's how I started. Didn't do me no harm."

Hattie Paige, the only woman on the board, snorted. "Depends on where you're sitting. You're an old coot, Eustace Farley. Always have been."

Eustace harrumphed, but no one paid attention.

1

"No teacher . . . no qualified teacher . . . is gonna want to spend nine months teaching in a burg like Flintrock," Norton said. "We ain't got nothing the big cities have."

"We can match any salary she names," Luke spoke for the first time.

"Money's not the only issue," Hattie said. "There's the isolation, the winters, the fact that there are no young people. A woman, a young woman, is going to want young men to court her." The old-fashioned phrasing drew a half smile from Luke.

It disappeared as all eyes turned to focus on him.

He barely suppressed a groan. Sometimes he felt like the only bachelor in the whole state of Montana. How many times had well-meaning friends tried to set him up with a niece, a sister, an out-of-state visitor?

"We don't want some flighty young gal who's going to up and get married at the drop of a hat," Eustace said. "We want someone stable, someone who's going to be around for the long haul."

Luke privately agreed. A sensible woman. He could see her now. Sensible shoes, sensible hair, sensible ideas. He was pragmatist enough to know they'd be lucky to attract even one qualified applicant. He loved his hometown, but he wasn't blind to its faults. He also knew enough of the world to realize it wouldn't appeal to everyone.

They were fighting to save the town's school. Old

Mrs. Winters, who had been a fixture at Flintrock's school for the last twenty-five years, had left at the end of the summer to go live with her widowed sister. If they couldn't find a teacher willing to take on the thirty-plus children of all different grades, the town would be forced to bus the kids to the county school, forty miles away.

Luke knew there were many who thought such a school was an anachronism, as out-of-date as high-buttoned shoes and bustles. But there were just as many—himself included—who believed in keeping the town's children close to home.

Flintrock's school was a mainstay of the community. Take it away, and he feared the whole town would start to crumble. He'd seen it happen in other small towns.

He didn't aim to let it happen here.

"The bottom line is that we need a teacher," he said evenly, determined to ignore the stares. "It's up to us to find one."

The rest of the board agreed.

As president of the school board, Luke was assigned the job of finding a teacher.

Back at the Falling Star Ranch, he slumped into the chair behind his desk. With more resignation than enthusiasm, he shoved away the weariness that cloaked him like a heavy blanket and concentrated on the task at hand. He scribbled out an ad and faxed it to all major newspapers in the northwest. He didn't have time for interviewing schoolteachers, he thought wearily. He didn't have time for all that had to be done now.

Ranching required constant work—cattle needed to be rounded up, winter wheat needed to be planted, fences needed to be checked, repaired, checked again. But he'd accepted the responsibility and he didn't shirk what he'd promised to do.

A quick glance at his desk produced a tired sigh. Bills, bills, and more bills. Slowly, he was paying them off, but he had a long road ahead of him.

He was tired, he thought. Worn down and worn out, like a horse rode hard and put away wet. Absently, he rubbed the back of his neck. The pain there was pretty much constant these days, the sort of ache brought on by too much worry and not enough of everything else.

For now, he shoved the pile of bills away. He had a family waiting for him.

A family.

The words still had the power to thrill him. And scare him to death. Two little girls depended upon him, and he didn't intend on letting them down. A fierce tenderness rushed over him. He'd never known he could feel that way—about anyone. But Annie and Ruth had found their way into his life . . . and into his heart.

They were there to stay, a precious legacy from

his brother, Dan. A coil of pain spiked, then settled in his heart as memories of his brother crowded into his mind. He tamped it down.

His nieces were waiting.

Meghan Sullivan had two suitcases, pitifully few references, and a heart full of determination. She didn't believe in luck, except what she made on her own. So what was she doing in Flintrock, Montana, applying for a teaching position that sounded like something out of a grade-B western?

The answer wasn't hard to find. For the first time in her life, she was doing something for herself, by herself, depending on no one but herself.

It felt good, she decided. Independence. She could practically taste it. She was twenty-six years old, but she'd never known the heady sensation of being on her own. Sheltered, some would say. Smothered, she called it.

She straightened her skirt, adjusted the collar of her jacket, and shored up her faltering courage—she had a feeling she was going to need it. This job interview was the key to her future.

Meeting her prospective employer at his home had come as a surprise. Maybe that was the way things were done out here.

The scenery had stolen her breath. *Magnificent* didn't begin to describe it. *Majestic* came closer. She was accustomed to the beauty of the northwest, but nothing had prepared her for the sight of mountains pushing their way through the clouds and a sky so big that it seemed to go on forever.

She let out the breath she hadn't realized she was holding and looked around. The trees climbing the mountains, though still green, hinted at the color that would soon gild their leaves in autumn splendor.

The house suited the land. Fashioned out of silver aged cedar and native stone, it melded with its surroundings. Only when she looked closer did she notice the signs of neglect. The pines towering above the house, nature's sentinels, snagged her attention. With a backdrop like that, peeling paint and splintered wood hardly mattered.

Meghan climbed steps made of slabs of stone, which led to massive double doors. She lifted the brass knocker and took the next step to a new life. The door swung open, and she came face-to-face with the biggest man she'd ever encountered.

Luke MacAllister was six-feet-four of Montana cowboy. Tall as she was, Meghan had to tip her head back to meet his gaze. Eyes the color of the fog rolling in over the ocean stared back at her.

"Mr. MacAllister?" She stuck out her hand. "I'm Meghan Sullivan."

"Ms. Sullivan." A calloused hand swallowed her own.

She felt herself subjected to a thorough inspection that made no attempt to be anything other than what it was. She had the uneasy feeling she didn't measure up.

"You're not what I had in mind," he said bluntly.

Though she'd expected it, hearing the words took her breath away.

The temptation was strong to take a step back so that she didn't have to tilt her head quite so far to meet his gaze, but she held her ground. She hadn't come this far to be turned away. Not without a fight.

She let her gaze slide down the length of him. There wasn't an ounce of extra flesh on him, she noted. Nor an ounce of softness. His eyes were as hard as the rugged mountains where he made his home.

Well, he'd find that Meghan Sullivan didn't run. She squared her shoulders and gave him a cool look. "Do you always make decisions without knowing the facts?" She didn't give him time to answer, but handed him a folder containing her résumé and references. Arms folded across her chest, she waited.

He gestured to a chair. She shook her head, preferring to stand.

"You don't have much experience," he said at last.

"I can do the job," she said quietly. "All I want is a chance."

He fired questions at her. She answered them as best she could, puzzled by some, amused by others, offended by a few.

How did she like cold weather?

Could she handle herself in a classroom made up of students of all different ages?

Did she have a problem with long winters?

When could she start?

—All right.

—Yes.

—No.

—Right away.

He scarcely gave her time to breathe before shooting off more questions.

''You've got yourself a job,'' he said at last.

She expelled a breath she hadn't known she was holding. ''Thank you.''

''Don't thank me. You can't know what you've taken on.'' He didn't give her time to respond to that. Not that she had a response at any rate. She was too busy reeling from an interview MacAllister-style.

He named a salary. Not a lot, but it included the use of a cottage. It wasn't the money she was interested in anyway. What she wanted—what she needed—was a job. A real, honest-to-goodness job that she'd earned on her own.

Now that she had it, she could afford to relax. She took her time looking around, grateful for an opportunity to turn her attention anywhere but toward the compelling man who'd just finished grilling her.

Wide plank floors gleamed gold with polish and

sunlight. Overstuffed furniture, heavy, sturdy, and comfortably shabby, invited you to make yourself at home. Antiques cozied up to a stereo system. Pictures, yellowed with age, of stern-faced ancestors lined the walls.

A real home, Meghan thought. Not a picture-perfect house designed by a professional decorator like the one where she'd grown up. But a home graced with love and clutter. A pair of roller skates had been left by the front door. Picture books mingled with ranching magazines on a scarred coffee table. A stuffed bear sprawled in an easy chair, his bedraggled state a mute testimony that he was a member of the family. Brown eyes stared back at her from a matted yellow fur face.

Unable to help herself, she skimmed a finger over a ratty ear. The soft material curled around her finger.

''That's Taffy.''

Flushing, she straightened and turned. Luke's gaze rested on her, quizzical and slightly challenging.

A smile twitched at her lips. ''It fits.'' Her stuffed animals had been pink and white and immaculate. Once they showed signs of wear, they'd been discarded. ''He looks like he's well loved.'' She flushed at the wistfulness in her voice.

''He's family,'' Luke said simply.

"Uncle Luke." A small whirlwind erupted into the room and threw herself at Luke.

Meghan had a feeling she'd just met Taffy's owner.

He stooped to swing the little girl into his arms and then tossed her over his shoulder. "Where did Annie go?" he asked, pretending to look around. "I can't find her anywhere."

"I'm here, Uncle Luke," his niece said.

"Where?"

"Down here." Upside-down, she tugged at his shirt until he swung her back around to settle her against his shoulder, her arm winding around his neck. They had obviously been through the routine many times before.

After he kissed her and was subjected to a wet, smacking kiss in return, he said, "Annie, this is Ms. Sullivan."

The little girl gave Meghan a radiant smile. "You're gonna be my teacher. Right?"

Meghan felt her lips curve in response. "Right."

Annie MacAllister was as fair as her uncle was dark. Blond curls framed a cherubic face dusted with freckles and what looked like the remains of a peanut butter and jelly sandwich. Only her gray eyes declared her relationship to Luke.

Luke's expression softened into one of genuine pleasure as he held the little girl close. Meghan felt herself warming to him. The man obviously doted on his niece. For a moment . . . a fraction of a moment really . . . she tasted the sour tang of envy. Envy of what they shared.

She mentally kicked herself for letting old memories, old hurts sneak up on her. She was a grown woman, for heaven's sake. Witnessing the love between the man and the little girl had opened up old wounds, wounds that had yet to heal over with scar tissue.

She pushed the past away and concentrated on the present. She was here to do a job, not dwell on the family she'd dreamed of and never had.

He wasn't given time to speculate on it. Annie was demanding to get down.

"Can I ride the pony today?" she asked when he set her down.

"Not today, honey. I've got to get Ms. Sullivan settled."

Another girl, about nine or ten, wandered into the room.

Luke brushed a kiss on her forehead before gesturing to Meghan. "Ruth, meet Ms. Sullivan. Your teacher." He laid a hand on her shoulder, which she shrugged off. A glimmer of pain flickered across his face. Meghan wasn't given time to wonder over it as he completed the introductions. "Meghan, my other niece, Ruth."

Ruth MacAllister looked at Meghan with too-old eyes and an unsmiling mouth.

"I'm glad to meet you, Ruth." Meghan held out her hand, only to drop it when it was ignored.

The girl's frown deepened.

She's hurting, Meghan thought. She wanted to pull the little girl close and hug her until she felt better, but she didn't have the right.

"Can you ride?" Ruth directed the challenge at Meghan.

"A little." If she counted riding lessons at a private riding academy more than a dozen years ago.

Ruth rolled her eyes. "Everyone rides here. Even Annie."

Meghan knew she'd failed a test. She prayed she'd fare better on future ones. That there'd be more wasn't in doubt. She was on trial here. In more ways than one.

She lifted her chin. She wasn't going to be run off. Not by Luke MacAllister or his niece. Not by anyone.

Ruth grabbed her little sister's hand. "Come on, Annie. We're out of here."

Annie gave Meghan a last smile before following her sister out of the room.

Luke ran a hand through his hair. "Sorry about that. Ruth tends to be pretty protective of Annie."

"What . . ." Meghan hesitated. She didn't have any right asking personal questions. On the other hand, she needed to know the children she'd be teaching. "What about their parents?"

"They died. Car accident." The words, clipped to the point of rudeness, dared her to offer sympathy.

When she thought he wasn't going to elaborate, he added, "We're still adjusting."

"I understand." A reluctant admiration stirred within her. Raising two small girls on his own couldn't be easy.

"I think you do at that." He studied her with frankly appraising eyes. Hair the color of ripe wheat fell in rippling waves past her shoulders. A hint of humor warmed her lips. But it was her eyes that caught and held his attention. Brown, they made him think of freshly turned earth. For many, the image wouldn't be attractive. For a man who made his living from that same earth, it was incredibly appealing. Mentally, he shook himself. He had no business thinking of the new schoolteacher in those terms. No business at all.

"You'll want to see your house," he said.

"Please."

Outside, he noticed a late-model sedan. He chuckled to himself, wondering how it would survive the rough roads crisscrossing the county. He climbed into a battered pickup, and with Meghan following in her own car, drove the short distance to the small house that had belonged to his father's aunt.

On the edge of town, it was close to the school and the few stores that Flintrock boasted. He'd done what he could to make it welcoming—stocked the refrigerator, hired a cleaning crew to wipe away years of neglect, even cleared a small plot in back in case the teacher had a mind to plant some bulbs.

"It's not much," he warned.

"It's charming." Yellow with white shutters, the cottage was something out of a storybook. A wicker fence and flower garden completed the picture. She climbed from the car before Luke could help her out.

She flung open the front door and looked around. It was cozy, she decided. Snug. Cozy. Perfect. As far removed from the house where she'd spent most of her life as it was possible to be.

A braided rug for the floor, she thought. And color. Lots of color. She could see it now. Books and pictures and plants and all the touches that made a house a home.

A home. The words settled around her heart with a sweet warmth that was as foreign as was the cottage. But right.

She itched to get started. But first she had to thank her landlord and employer. She turned.

"It's beautiful."

"If you need anything—"

"I'll let you know."

He took his leave soon after that. She wasn't sorry to see him go. Luke MacAllister unsettled her in more ways than one.

She was eager to explore her new home. A narrow staircase led to the second story. The main bedroom boasted a four-poster bed and dormer windows. A second, smaller bedroom would make a perfect study, she decided. A place to grade papers, to read. Or to dream.

A tiny bathroom tucked beneath the eaves charmed her. A clawfoot tub claimed most of the floor space. She didn't care. Delighted with it, she ran a hand over the white porcelain.

By nighttime, she'd unpacked and set out her few belongings—a china doll that had once been her mother's, a watercolor she'd found at a flea market, a basket of yarn with a half-finished afghan inside.

The rest she'd collect one piece at a time. The idea of decorating her home just as she wanted was an exhilarating one.

The sounds of the house settled around her, comforting, soothing sounds. They wrapped themselves around her as she fell asleep.

"Miss Mommy and Daddy," Annie murmured. Sleep slurred her words as she clutched Taffy to her.

Luke brushed a kiss across her forehead. When he assured himself she would stay asleep, he slumped beside her bed, head bowed. He tried to summon the energy to get up and drag himself to bed. Instead, he stayed by Annie's bed and listened to the soothing rhythm of her breathing.

Dan and Christine had been gone for nearly a

year. A year in which he'd tried to be both father and mother to his orphaned nieces.

Together, the three of them were becoming a family. Slowly, the girls were starting to trust him. Annie, at five, had adjusted to the changes with a minimum of trouble. Ruth, who had just turned ten two weeks ago, was still waking with nightmares.

There'd been no question that he would take in Dan's two children. They were family, and Luke believed in family.

That he and Dan had never agreed on anything didn't lessen Luke's love for his brother. Or his children. Ruth and Annie were all he had left of Dan. He'd do his best for them, just as he'd tried to for their father.

Before his father's death, the old man had extracted a promise from Luke that he'd look out for Daniel.

"Your brother's not like you," his pa had said. "He's a dreamer. I ain't saying he ain't smart. But he's got his head in the clouds. I'm dividing the ranch between you. Not because it's the smart thing to do. But because it's fitting. It ain't fair to you," he added almost as an afterthought.

Luke started to protest, but his pa ignored him.

"Don't think I don't know that you've been carrying most of the weight around here. Have for a long time. Even before I took sick." A fit of coughing robbed him of his voice, making the next words come in gasps. "Take care of Danny. He needs you. He won't let on, but he does."

His father had died shortly after that. Luke had done his best for Dan. Or thought he had. Maybe if he'd tried harder, if he'd been more supportive, if . . . A half smile edged his mouth. His pa had been fond of saying that what-ifs were as useless as a cow without teats.

Annie stirred, settled. Luke smoothed back a stray curl from her face, smiling when she popped a thumb into her mouth. She'd given up the habit during the daytime—peer pressure, five-year-old style, had seen to that, but she occasionally sucked her thumb at night.

"Pa," he whispered into the night. "What do I do now?"

Chapter Two

Meghan reviewed her first day of school and decided she'd passed. There'd been no apples on her desk. But no frogs either.

Meghan Sullivan had no illusions about herself—she was too tall, too thin, too ordinary for beauty—just as she had no illusions about why she'd been given the teaching position. Her teaching experience was limited, as were her references. Two jobs, both in small, private schools, were the extent of her background.

No, she'd been hired for one reason and one reason only. She was willing to move to the back of beyond—in other words, Flintrock, Montana.

She didn't delude herself into believing that teaching children from five different grades at one time would be easy. It sounded like something from a century ago. But those children deserved an education, the best she could give them. She didn't intend on letting them down.

Her chin lifted in resolve. She would prove she was equal to the task, she vowed silently. And she would prove something else as well. She would accomplish it on her own. Without her father's influence or wealth. Wasn't that why she'd come here, to a town so small it didn't even rate a blip on the map?

She would make a good teacher, she promised, and, if she were lucky, a life for herself as well. And what better time to begin a new life than fall, with its gaudy colors and grand expectations? It was the season of new clothes, unmarked notebooks, and freshly sharpened pencils without any teeth marks gnawed in the wood.

She gathered up her things and pushed open the door. The sheer beauty that confronted her caused her to gasp in pleasure.

Even at late afternoon, the day was as bright as a child's paint box of colors, the sky so blue it hurt the eyes to stare into it, the landscape done up fancy with autumn hues. It was nature at its best.

In the distance, snow topped the mountains, dribbling down them like whipped cream atop a hot fudge sundae. The analogy pleased her, and she grinned at the imagined look on Luke MacAllister's face if she were to tell him of it. He was a no-

nonsense man, one who probably didn't indulge in fanciful notions.

A frown pleated her forehead. Just when and how had she allowed herself to become so darned aware of Luke as a man? She'd met him less than seventy-two hours ago, had seen him only once since the interview. So why did she find herself thinking about him at odd hours?

Because she had no answer to that—no acceptable answer anyway—she pushed it from her mind. She decided to take the long way home. Flintrock was her home now. It was time she made it so.

The town was postcard-pretty, with tidy houses, a town square complete with the requisite statue of a local hero in its center, and one traffic light. A hardware store, ladies' boutique, and beauty emporium-cum-drugstore made up the business district. A movie theater featuring a year-old film provided entertainment.

She thought of downtown Seattle, the dazzling array of restaurants and espresso bars, the plays and concerts, the aquariums and museums, and decided she didn't miss them. Things didn't make a place a home. People did.

A woman with a toddler in tow gave her a friendly "Good afternoon" and a smile. Two teenage girls waved. Meghan waved back, feeling at ease in a way she'd never felt in her own hometown.

She found a small diner tucked between the hardware store and the library. An ancient soft drink machine hummed outside.

Her stomach grumbled noisily, a reminder that she'd skipped breakfast this morning in the excitement of starting a new job. The rich yeasty aroma of fresh bread enticed her to walk inside. A pretty girl arrived to take her order, and Meghan asked for a cinnamon roll and a cup of tea.

The roll, as large as a small loaf of bread, lived up to her expectations. She bit into it, savoring the airy texture and caramel sweetness.

"I see you've discovered Flintrock's claim to fame."

She looked up to find Luke MacAllister grinning down at her.

"Belle's cinnamon rolls." He folded his long legs into the opposite seat and signaled the waitress. Within minutes, she arrived with two rolls and a glass of milk.

"They know me here," he said simply, in response to Meghan's raised brow.

Fascinated, she watched as he polished off both rolls before she had finished only half of hers. That much man had a lot to fill up, she thought.

"What do you think of our town?"

"I love it."

A slow grin worked its way across his lips, deepening the dimple at the corner of his mouth. Once again, she experienced a tingling awareness.

An older woman burst through the doors. A wide smile upon her frankly lined face, she trotted toward their booth at a determined pace and stuck out her hand. "Hattie Paige. And you must be our new schoolteacher."

"Meghan Sullivan, Mrs. Paige."

"Hattie."

"Hattie." The name suited the woman. Meghan felt a matching smile tug at her lips.

"Good to see you too, Hattie," Luke said wryly.

"I'll get to you in a minute," she said. "I want time to get to know Meghan here. Go on." She shooed him off with a wave of her hand.

"Good luck," he whispered to Meghan on his way out.

She barely had time to wonder what he meant by that before Hattie started in on her.

Meghan found herself interrogated with gentle relentlessness. If she'd thought Luke had subjected her to a grueling interview, it was only because she hadn't yet met Hattie. Twenty minutes later, Hattie had extracted everything about Meghan except her blood type.

"You're going to do us proud," Hattie said.

Hattie's words echoing through her mind, Meghan started home. She didn't mind the walk. It gave her time to sort her thoughts. She'd made a good start, she decided. Now it was time to buckle down. She had a teacher's first-day-of-school ritual on her agenda tonight: grading ''What I Did on My Summer Vacation'' papers.

She'd expanded on the traditional theme to ''What I Learned on My Summer Vacation.'' The essays were hilarious and serious in turn, she discovered some hours later. Some were so full of life and joy that she felt herself living through a trip to the Florida Everglades that one boy had described in detail, including an up-close and personal encounter with an alligator. Others were so poignant that they brought tears to her eyes, like that of one little girl who recounted the details of her parents' divorce.

It was a way of getting to know her kids. *Her kids.* The words stuck in her mind. And in her heart.

Her kids.

Meghan had quickly adapted to the rituals of small-town living. Sundays meant dressing up—hats and gloves required—and going to church. This Sunday the preacher gave a fiery sermon about the wages of sin. The Sunday school children sang. The ladies' auxiliary served coffee and donuts following the meeting.

More often than not, a family in town invited her over for Sunday dinner. In the city, accepting invitations from students' families wasn't encouraged. Nor were they offered. Here, it was not only encouraged; it was expected.

Pot roast with new potatoes. Fried chicken and

mashed potatoes. Even buffalo steak . . . with fried potatoes. She'd tried them all. She groaned, remembering the desserts and thinking about the extra pounds she'd probably put on. With more than a little pride at stake, the townswomen had outdone themselves—pineapple upside-down cake, chocolate cream pie, blueberry cobbler.

It was but one more part of her new life.

Today's invitation from Annie to join the family on a picnic wasn't immediately picked up by her uncle. Or by Ruth. Meghan was on the verge of refusing when Luke gave his slow smile.

"Please," he added.

"I'd like that," she said.

Luke drove past the outskirts of town, following a rutted road that led to a wooded area. "Time to hoof it," he said. He hefted the hamper while the girls carried blankets.

Within minutes, they came to a meadow, nestled between stands of pines. Shaded by the massive trees, it was still green. Meghan felt like she'd stumbled onto a jewel hidden deep in the forest. Sunlight gilded the day with nature's own brand of magic. She grabbed hold of it and held on tight.

The picnic basket yielded thick slabs of roast beef on homemade bread, baked beans, a bag of chips, chocolate-chip cookies, and a thermos of lemonade.

"Thank goodness," she murmured.

Luke gave her a quizzical look.

"No potatoes."

He chuckled. "Too many Sunday dinners," he guessed.

She nodded. "Don't get me wrong. I love 'em. But I've had so many potatoes, I'm starting to sprout."

Throughout the meal, Meghan noticed the casual way Luke had of letting the girls know that he loved them.

She liked the way he touched them so easily. Some men had trouble showing affection. A quick hug, a pat on the shoulder, went a long way toward making many problems go away.

The screech of a prairie falcon had her looking up. The sight of the bird gliding through the cloud-dusted sky transfixed her. She watched as it swooped to pounce upon a rabbit, then soar upward once more, the prey caught in its talons.

Her gaze shifted to the man at her side. He was as much a part of his environment as the falcon, which even now was screaming in triumph at its catch. He belonged here.

"It's beautiful," she said.

"Most city folk get put off by the idea of wild animals hunting their food."

"Maybe I'm not most city folk."

He gave her one of those enigmatic looks that left her wondering what he was thinking. "Maybe you're not."

She wanted to believe that he was beginning to see that she was herself, not some stereotype of what he believed a city girl to be.

He curled a knuckle under her chin and tilted her face to his. "You'll do."

The thank-you she'd been about to say died before she could give voice to it. *You'll do*. What did he mean by that? The tender feelings she'd been entertaining abruptly vanished. How did he propel her from exasperation to excitement to anger so quickly, so effortlessly?

The man was clearly impossible. She opened her mouth to tell him just that.

He forestalled her by pointing to the sky. "See it?"

She lifted her gaze. An eagle soared overhead, its wingspan easily four or more feet.

"Someday maybe you'll see the white eagle."

"The what?"

"The white eagle. Legend has it if a person sees it and makes a wish, it'll come true."

"Have you ever seen it?"

The expression in his eyes went flat. "I don't believe in legends. Or dreams coming true."

"Of course not." But she wondered. What had stolen his dreams? What or who? She searched for the courage to ask him and found it wanting.

Coward, she berated herself. Luke had given her the opportunity to learn more about him, and she didn't have the guts to follow through with it. It wasn't difficult to understand why: She didn't want to destroy the fragile peace they'd reached today.

Avoiding confrontations had become second nature to her. Wasn't that why she'd put up with her father's bullying for as long as she had? To keep the peace, at any cost.

The realization that she was doing the same thing with Luke tainted her mouth with self-recrimination. She wasn't the same woman who'd let others scare her off.

Before she could talk herself out of it, she asked, "Why?"

"Dreams are for fools," he said. "Or those too young to know any different. My brother was a dreamer. Or he used to be."

"Used to be?"

"My sister-in-law crushed his dreams almost before their first year together was over."

The closed look that shadowed his face nearly stopped her next question. "And you? What about your dreams?"

"I told you. Dreams belong to fools. It doesn't matter anymore. They're both dead now."

His brother and sister-in-law were dead, but she had a feeling it still mattered very much. "I'm sorry." She winced at the inadequacy of the words.

He pulled back.

Hurt flared in her eyes at his withdrawal.

"Time to get back," he said, and started packing the hamper.

"Luke—"

"I got work to do." The instant the words were out of his mouth, he wanted to snatch them back.

"Uncle Luke?" The baby-soft words stopped Luke in his tracks. "Are you mad at Meghan?" Annie's small face, dusted with cookie crumbs, looked up at him.

"No, Pumpkin. I'm not mad at Meghan."

"Who're you mad at then?"

Who was he mad at? Himself, he guessed. He wanted more than simple friendship from Meghan. But he had no right. One of nature's miracles saved him from answering. "Shh." He pointed to the edge of the meadow.

"Wh..." Meghan saw them, the doe and her fawn, their subtle colors blending with their surroundings. "They're beautiful." The words came out as the barest whisper.

Suddenly alert, the doe lifted her head. A nudge to her baby and they were gone, as silently as they'd appeared.

"They smelled us." Luke's voice broke through her frozen wonder.

Impulsively, she turned to him and threw her arms around him. "Thank you for bringing me here." Embarrassed, she started to back away when his hands settled at her waist, holding her against him.

Luke watched the play of emotions across her features. Her face was wonderfully expressive. He wondered if she knew just how much of herself she revealed in her eyes. He doubted it. The lady didn't give much away, not if she could help it at any rate.

"It was my pleasure." And it was. It was pure pleasure just watching her. And smelling her. She smelled as fresh as the mountain air. No perfume interfered with the soap-and-water scent of her. She not only felt good against him, but *right*. With some surprise, Luke realized this was the first time he'd ever known simple contentment in a woman's company.

He tried to remember the last time he'd taken a whole day off. Even Sundays were usually spent working following church services. The pleasure he read in the girls' eyes was enough to convince him to make this a habit. And then there was Meghan. A day in her company wasn't exactly a hardship. To please himself, he took her hand, stroking the soft skin on the underside of her wrist.

Meghan tried to ignore the long, slow tug of pleasure as he ran his thumb across her wrist.

Annie pulled at Meghan's skirt. "Meghan?"

Meghan looked down to see Annie staring up at her, eyes wide and wondering.

"Do you like it when Uncle Luke holds your hand?"

How was she supposed to answer that?

"Well, do you?" Annie persisted.

At a loss, Meghan turned to Luke.

He grinned at her. "Do you?"

She got a grip on her sense of humor. "What's not to like?"

Luke gave her a quizzical look. Annie grinned. And Meghan decided she might be a little bit in love with both of them. Ruth stayed outside the circle. That brought a small frown to Meghan's lips. Someday, she promised herself, she'd find a way to unlock the girl's heart.

A laugh bubbled inside her, warm and comfortable. How did he do it—turn her knees to jelly with his caresses one moment and have her laughing the next? She didn't bother worrying over it. Right now, she was content to accept what she'd found.

The sun was riding low in the sky, all bleeding colors and fiery light. Montana sunsets held their own kind of beauty, Meghan had discovered.

She'd completed her first month as Flintrock's teacher. Noise and confusion had reigned for the first couple of days as she'd learned names, who liked to show off, who needed extra attention. For their part, the children had seemed to take to her, laughing with her when she'd discovered a family of raccoons nestled behind the schoolhouse, encouraging her when she'd struggled over the Native-American names of some of her students.

A frown inched its way between her brows. Ruth MacAllister was the exception. Ruth was undoubtedly intelligent. Her work gave her away, even though she refused to participate in class. But she kept herself aloof from everyone, everyone but Annie, that is.

Meghan promised herself she'd find a way to reach Luke's older niece. She hadn't seen much of him since the picnic. She ignored the odd flash of disappointment she'd felt.

She drove the short distance to the Falling Star, wishing she had something with four-wheel drive instead of the impractical luxury sedan her father had insisted she buy several years ago. She had her first official request to make.

"They're in there." Juanita pointed to the den.

Meghan had met Juanita when she came to pick up Ruth and Annie from school. From Annie, she'd learned that Juanita had been with the family since Luke was a boy. Now she cared for his nieces.

"They?"

Juanita only smiled. "You go on in."

Gently, Meghan eased open the door. Her eyes took a quick impression of the room—rough-hewn cedar walls, deep-cushioned leather chairs, a slab of a desk. The room was as big and forbidding as the man himself. Furniture was scaled to fit the size of the owner. A Native-American mask occupied the center of the far wall, while a brightly woven rug covered the floor. A man's room. But it was the scene before her that caused a smile to curl at her lips.

Luke and Annie were on the floor. Squealing, she jumped on him while he pretended to cower away. Annie tackled him, her small hands easily caught by his big ones. High-pitched laughter mingled with deeper rumbles as the two of them tussled and wrestled. After an initial hesitation, Ruth joined in, jumping into the fray with more enthusiasm than Meghan had ever seen from her.

Unashamedly, Meghan took advantage of the opportunity to watch. She wasn't surprised. Luke had shown how much he loved his nieces. Seeing him lie on the floor and let the girls climb all over him only confirmed what she'd known. She liked men like that. And she already liked Luke. Liked him too much.

"Enough, enough," he begged when both girls sat on his stomach and tickled him.

"Cry uncle," Ruth demanded, zeroing in on his ribs with her fingers.

"Uncle."

"Me, too," Annie demanded.

"Uncle." He flipped both of them over and retaliated until all three of them had dissolved in giggles.

"Okay, you two terrors. Let me up. An old man like your uncle can't be rolling around on the floor."

"You aren't old, Uncle Luke," Annie said loyally. "Not *real* old, anyway."

"Thanks, Pumpkin." He got to his feet, pulling both girls up with him.

Annie spied Meghan and threw her arms around her legs, hugging her fiercely. Ruth contented herself with her usual frown. They darted off when Juanita appeared to announce she'd just whipped up a cake and would anyone want to lick the bowl.

Luke lifted his head, his gaze connecting with Meghan's.

"Meghan." His smile started in his eyes and worked its way down to his mouth.

It was the first time he'd used her name. Meghan felt it shimmer over her in the softest of caresses. It sounded different coming from him. Strong. And yet it had an intensely feminine ring to it that she instinctively responded to. Her breath hitched in her throat.

She admired his face in the strong light of the sun, streaming through the full-length windows. Unapologetically angled, it was not handsome, not in a conventional sense. His features were too strong, too compelling for pretty-boy good looks like those of the men her father had foisted upon her.

No, his face would never be termed handsome. But it was attractive in a way that invited the viewer to take a second . . . and a third look. It hinted at the strength that was so much a part of him.

It was his eyes, though, that captivated her. Eyes that saw everything and mirrored nothing inside him. Eyes that could warm with love as he gazed at his nieces or darken to the color of the ocean in the middle of a storm when he was angry.

At the moment, they settled on her with such intensity that she had to resist the desire to squirm.

She took a step back. Then another. Her breath came easier now. With an effort, she steadied her breathing and tried to remember why she'd come to see him.

''The school.''

Apparently she'd spoken the words aloud, for he looked at her expectantly.

''We need . . .'' *What did she need?* The matter, so pressing only minutes ago, had vanished from her mind with a completeness that startled her.

She focused in an effort to distract her thoughts from Luke. ''Computers. We need more computers.'' She said the words a little too loudly in an effort to cover her nervousness.

''We ordered twelve new ones last year.''

It wasn't a no. She took courage in that.

''I know. But we're starting to write books. I want each child—''

''You mean *you're* writing a book and the kids are helping.''

''I mean the children are writing their own books.''

He looked intrigued. "All of them?"

"All of them."

"How does a six-year-old write a book?"

"Some of the books are really short. Just a couple of pages. The important thing is that each kid writes something. When we're all done, we'll invite the families to come to our book fair."

"You believe in starting off big, don't you?"

"Anything wrong with that?"

He didn't answer directly, but scribbled a note. "You'll have them by next week."

She stared at him in disbelief. "Just like that?"

"Just like that. What's the matter? What did you expect I'd say?"

She shook her head. "I don't know."

"How do they do things in that fancy school you came from?"

"Requisition forms. In triplicate. After that, I get a letter saying that my order is delayed. A few months later, if I'm lucky, I might get what I wanted."

A smile lit his eyes. "I'm beginning to get the picture."

Encouraged, she launched into a description of all the projects she had planned. "You see, I want to—"

"Why don't you quit trying so hard?"

"Sorry." She smiled faintly. "Old habits."

"Give 'em up."

She thought about it. He had her pegged all right. Trying too hard and wanting too much.

"Not the writing project."

"No, not that. I can't wait to read Annie and Ruth's books."

"You really care about the children here, don't you?"

His eyes darkened to the color of smoke. Fire-spitting smoke. "You thought I didn't?"

"I didn't know," she said frankly. "Now I do."

"You can count on it."

And she could. Luke MacAllister was a man a woman could count on.

"Luke?"

"Yeah?"

"Thanks."

She took herself off after that, leaving him to wonder about a woman so determined to prove herself— and just who she was trying to prove herself to.

Luke had planned on spending the evening filling out quarterly reports. His good intentions never got past first base. Meghan's face kept superimposing itself over the figures.

It would have been better, he thought, if she'd been closer to the woman of his imagination. Sensible shoes, scraped-back hair, no-nonsense clothes, and a mouth like a persimmon.

He recognized the conjured-up picture as ridiculous, a stereotype that was out-of-date a century ago. Still, it had been a comforting one.

Meghan Sullivan was a fascinating combination of toughness and vulnerability. The reality of her was too unsettling for his peace of mind. He thought of the excitement, the anticipation that had radiated from her in almost palpable waves this afternoon as she'd described her project. He'd felt the energy arc through the air, forming a bridge between them.

The town was lucky to have her, he reminded himself. Unquestionably competent, thoroughly professional, she brought one additional ingredient to the job—she genuinely cared about her students. He'd heard from parents that their children were responding to her.

They deserved the best. And Ms. Meghan Sullivan was just that. He wondered how he was going to keep ignoring the attraction he felt for her.

The hour was crowding midnight by the time Luke started upstairs. A yawn pulled at his mouth. He headed to his room and stopped short when he saw Annie running down the hallway.

''What're you doing up, Pumpkin?'' He bent to scoop the little girl into his arms.

''Can't sleep.'' Annie clung to his neck.

''A bad dream?''

She shook her head.

''What's wrong then?''

''Ruth's crying.''

"She is?" Luke frowned.

"Won't stop." Annie turned her face into his shoulder.

"I'll go and see what's wrong," he said, smoothing the hair back from her face. "Don't worry, honey."

Annie nodded, but didn't raise her head. Luke hugged her tightly. "Everything's going to be okay."

" 'Kay," she murmured sleepily.

Luke carried Annie to his bedroom and tucked her in the bed before going down the hallway to the girls' room. Muffled sobs caused him to stop outside the door. It wasn't the first time he'd been called to deal with Ruth's nightmares. She hadn't had one in the last few months, and he'd hoped she'd outgrown them. Apparently not.

He eased the door open. "Ruth? It's Uncle Luke."

The hallway light spilled into the room, chasing away the shadows. A small figure on the bed was curled into a fetal position. When he moved closer, he saw that she was still asleep.

He perched on the edge of the bed and shook her gently. "Ruth. Wake up, honey. It's all right."

A keening sound wrenched at his heart. He gathered her into his arms and held her close.

"Uncle Luke?"

"I'm here, sweetheart."

"What happened?"

"You were having a nightmare."

She rubbed her eyes. ''Was I? I don't remember.''

''Are you sure? You don't have to be afraid to tell me.''

''I was dreaming that Annie and I were in the car with Mom and Dad when it . . . you know.''

''I know.'' He waited for the lump in his throat to dissolve. ''But you weren't. You were right here with Juanita and me. Just like you are now.'' He rocked her back and forth, murmuring the kind of nonsense Juanita had when he'd been a small boy and unable to sleep. He continued to hold Ruth long after the gentle cadence of her breathing told him she was asleep.

Meghan frowned at the empty seat. Ruth Mac-Allister hadn't shown up for school for the second day in a row.

Meghan had the feeling anyone trying to befriend the little girl would have their work cut out for them. Ruth didn't wear her heart on her sleeve the way Annie did. She was like her uncle in that respect.

Meghan stopped at Annie's desk and hunkered down. ''Annie?''

''Uh-huh?'' Annie looked up, her eyes bright with pleasure and trust.

''Why isn't Ruth at school today?''

Some of the glow faded from Annie's face. ''She wasn't feeling so good.''

That could cover a multitude of reasons, Meghan thought. She cared about all her students, but she was worried about Ruth. For a ten-year-old girl, she was entirely too serious.

Of course, losing both her parents in a single stroke would be traumatic for any child. But Meghan sensed it was more than that. It was as if Ruth carried some secret inside her heart, a secret too terrible to voice aloud.

She'd called Luke, asking him to meet her after school. He'd sounded distracted, preoccupied. When he showed up at four looking exhausted and just a little irritated, she squared her shoulders, the small gesture reminding her that she had nothing to apologize for.

The man might not like what she had to say, but he had hired her to do a job. Right now that job meant talking with him about his niece. A child was in pain. Nothing else mattered.

"Please, have a seat. I'll be right with you." She turned to finish writing the next day's assignment on the chalkboard.

When she had finished, she found Luke sprawled on one of the pint-size chairs, head propped on his laced hands. Weariness—or worry—had etched hard lines into his face. Her heart turned over.

He lifted his head. For a moment, the tension and exhaustion were reflected in his eyes. But his jaw tightened, and the tiredness was washed away, making her wonder if she'd imagined the hint of vulnerability. She couldn't feel sorry for him, not when his lips flattened into a hard line and he met her gaze with an unreadable expression.

Her mind refused to focus and she shook her head slightly, trying to clear away the cobwebs.

"Ruth's been absent the last two days. I wanted to check on her. If she's sick, I can send her work home."

"She's not sick."

"Then why . . ."

"She's not sick, okay? I'll see she's there tomorrow."

"Is there something bothering her?"

"Are you saying I can't take care of my kids?" He half turned from her, his profile hard with anger.

Anger she'd put there. Well, that was too bad. Her chin lifted as determination flooded through her. It was time Luke MacAllister learned that she didn't back down. Not when one of her children needed help.

"You don't have to prove anything to me," she said. "I know how much you care about your nieces."

"Sorry. I had no call flying off the handle like that. It's been a . . . tough week." A sigh rippled from him.

There it was again. The weariness that she'd sensed minutes earlier. She steeled herself against offering the sympathy that welled up inside of her. Long minutes passed. It began to look as though he didn't intend on offering any explanations.

His anger evaporated along with his energy. He slumped back in his chair. "Ruth's going through a rough patch," he said at last. He gave a short laugh. "We all are."

"I'm sorry," she said quietly. "It can't be easy for you, trying to take care of two little girls on your own."

"We manage," he said shortly.

"I didn't mean—" She let it go. "If there's anything you can think of that I can do, I'd appreciate your letting me know."

"She's been having nightmares," he said at last.

"Her parents?" She didn't ask a lot of useless questions, he thought with a flash of appreciation. Instead, she cut right to the heart of the problem.

"Yeah."

"How long ago since they . . ."

"Since they died? A little over a year."

"A year's a big part of a child's life."

He hadn't thought of it that way before. Ruth was barely ten. A year equaled a tenth of her lifetime. How did Meghan immediately grasp what he was only beginning to understand?

It was but one more piece of the puzzle of Meghan Sullivan. For a moment, he let himself wonder what it would be like to have someone special in his life. Someone to share the good times with, as well as the bad. Someone to laugh with, shed tears with . . . to love. Forcibly, he reminded himself that his relationship with Meghan was that of friends.

Friends.

Why did it sound so empty? Or leave him feeling so depressed?

Chapter Three

Early the next morning, Luke headed to the barn. A ride would smooth away the rough edges of a nearly sleepless night. The soft whickerings and pungent smell of horses soothed him as nothing else could.

"Hey there, fellow," he said, holding out an apple for his mount, a big gelding.

Bear whinnied in pleasure at the unexpected treat. Luke watched as the horse chomped down the apple in one bite.

"You feeling frisky this morning?" he asked, sidestepping as Bear tried to nip him. "Up for a ride?"

Another whinny answered in the affirmative.

Pink fingers of light poked their way through the

sky, a promise of the day to come. Clouds scuttled across the morning gray.

Luke took the ride from the valley up to the foot-hills at an easy pace. The cattle were fat and sassy, he noted with satisfaction. A few more weeks and he'd be cutting out the best for finishing in feedlots before winter. The others, he'd rotate between pastures, holding them for another year until they were at their peak.

No doubt about it, the ranch was prospering. Slowly, to be sure, but the signs were there. Fences were in good condition. He'd added a cash crop this year, built onto the barn, and even played with the idea of breeding a few quarter horses to use as cutting horses during roundup.

The drone of a plane overhead had him looking up. Someday, he vowed, someday, he'd have one of his own, a small Cessna maybe. A rancher could save days, maybe weeks, with a plane to survey the land. He already had his license. All he needed now was the cash.

Yeah, right, he thought. Like he had any extra cash. Money was something in short supply, and it didn't look like things were going to change anytime soon. Not with Daniel's debts still to pay off.

Some said he oughtn't to bother with his brother's debts. After all, they held, Luke hadn't been the one to marry a fancy wife and then go broke trying to keep her. But Daniel, dead or not, was a MacAllister. And MacAllisters paid their debts. It wasn't simply a question of honor. It was a matter of family. And family was all-important.

The air thinned as they climbed, the ground covered with boulders. Luke patted Bear's neck, reining him in slightly. The big gelding didn't like slowing the pace, even when the going got rough.

"Simmer down, boy," Luke murmured. "We're in no hurry."

He pulled up, to look over the valley below. To the east, the river lazily meandered. Wildflowers covered the hillsides, a bright blanket of color. Cows dotted the meadows, patches of brown and white against the summer-yellowed grass.

Luke scanned the horizon, hoping the clouds meant rain. Summer heat had sapped the land dry.

A rancher spent a good part of his life praying about rain. Too little meant drought; too much, flooding. Land baked hard by the sun for three months needed a gentle soaking. Too frequently, autumn storms pummeled the ground mercilessly. The parched earth had no chance to absorb the moisture, flooding the streams and riverbeds.

Ranching is for fools, his pa had said more than once. "You and me, son, we're fools for wanting to make our living from the land."

"Then why do we stay?" Luke had wanted to know.

''Because our roots are here. And our dreams.''

Lucas MacAllister had been born at the house, and his father before him. Luke's great-grandfather had built it at the turn of the century, back when the land was more wilderness than tamed.

His father had been gone for more than twelve years now, but Luke felt his presence every day.

Don't make a passel of promises, his pa had said more years ago than Luke cared to count. And make sure you keep the ones you do. It had been good advice then. It still was.

Lucas MacAllister had been a good man, honest as they came and so fair that folks had come from miles away to have him settle disputes. Though he'd left school after eighth grade and never set foot in a university, people had taken to calling him Judge. He had accepted the name with good nature and even better sense. He'd remained what he was—a simple man with no ambition other than to care for his family and the land entrusted to him.

He'd asked of his sons what he demanded of himself—hard work and honest dealings. That and respect for the land. Only once had Luke seen his father cry . . . when his wife walked out, leaving two young sons and no regrets. The sight of his pa crying had shaken the young Luke down to the core.

Yes, he'd been a good man, a great one, some had said. But he hadn't been much on experimentation.

If something worked in the past, that was good enough for him.

Luke had respected his pa and hadn't tried to change things during his lifetime. It had been time, though, to think forward, rather than backward. Over the years, Luke had set aside a thousand acres for small grains and built a silo to ferment his own alfalfa. Self-sufficiency was the name of the game.

With the price of cattle dipping, a smart man kept his options open. Luke figured himself to be a smart man.

A rancher had to diversify if he was to hold onto his land. Developers, citified vultures with three-piece suits and slicked-back hair, had their eye on the Falling Star. One had offered Luke top dollar for the ranch. It shamed him to own up to it, but he'd been tempted. Sorely tempted.

A couple of his neighbors had succumbed to the lure of quick money. He didn't blame them for cutting their losses and getting out. But he wouldn't be doing the same.

The land was his heritage, his link to the past, his passport to the future.

Luke had plowed whatever extra money he had— and there was precious little—back into the land.

Too little money and too little time. A rancher's lament.

When snow came, they'd drive the cattle down to the low meadow. An early blizzard could wipe out a herd grazing in the high country. But there was time yet, he thought.

He had learned to interpret nature's signs. A lifetime of ranch work had taught him how to *feel* the changes in the weather. It was a good life. He couldn't imagine living anywhere else.

How could anyone prefer the suffocation of the city, he wondered, where a person felt smothered with too many people, too many things? He recalled a recent trip to Billings. The streets clogged with cars and irate drivers, buildings a tawdry imitation of nature's own skyscraping mountains, houses stacked close together with scarcely a slice of sky between them.

He could hardly take a step without bumping into someone. It was a pretty enough city, he'd supposed, if you liked all the noise and confusion. The sheer number of people, where everyone seemed in some desperate rush to get somewhere other than where they were, had made him yearn for the quiet, lazy pace of Flintrock and the clean air that was perfumed by the scent of pines instead of exhaust fumes.

Of course, a city dweller might see things differently, might not feel the tug of the land, the freedom of the open range.

His thoughts turned to Meghan. Did she appreciate the beauty of the Big Sky country? Or was it just one big wilderness to her, the town quaint, the people quainter? The idea twisted in his gut. He clamped down on the direction his reflections had taken.

Irritated, he took off his hat, wiped the sweat from his forehead, and then jammed the hat back on his head before nudging Bear on. Elk had knocked over the fence bordering the north pasture—again. If he didn't get it repaired soon, the cattle would discover it and wander away. Dumb animals didn't know enough to stay where it was safe.

Despite his resolve, Meghan kept creeping into his thoughts. Why did he find himself thinking of her at odd moments? It didn't matter what he was doing— putting up fence, tending a sick calf, or working on the end-of-the-month reports, his mind conjured up pictures of her. The lady had invaded his thoughts to the point that he couldn't even trust himself shaving, for fear of cutting his face to pieces.

The acknowledgment had his lips tightening in annoyance. He wasn't a green boy to fall to pieces over a pair of pretty eyes and a soft mouth. There was something about her . . . something that defied the ruthless logic he applied to the rest of his life . . . something that he was powerless to resist.

He pushed the thought away, angry that he'd entertained it even for a moment. He'd set his course years ago; he wouldn't be changing it. Not even for a woman like Meghan.

He had no business wanting her, no business thinking about her. But still he did. Want her. Think about her. He was coming dangerously close to needing her.

An impatient whicker from Bear reminded him that they had work to do.

"You're right, boy," he murmured. "Enough daydreaming. Time to get to work."

When Luke showed up after school Friday afternoon, Meghan reined in her curiosity. A member of the school board, he was probably checking up on her. Well, she had nothing to hide.

"I hate to ask, but I need your help." The reluctance in his voice told her more than words just how he felt about asking for her help. "Juanita's daughter has just had her first baby . . . Juanita's first grandchild. She wants to be with them, but she won't leave if she thinks the girls need her. I've got a meeting in Billings with Dan's lawyer. It's likely to take a couple of days. I'd put it off, but there's a lot riding on it. I thought if I got someone to stay with Annie and Ruth . . ."

"You want me to come stay with them."

"Yeah."

It was killing him, she thought, having to depend on someone other than himself. The independence that was so much a part of him was now his enemy.

"I'd pay you, of course."

That had her chin lifting a notch. "Was it just so

much hype about people helping each other out in small towns?''

''No, but—''

''Then let me be a part of it. Please.''

That settled the matter.

The arrangements were simple enough. She'd take Ruth and Annie to school with her, bring them home, spend the night. Simple. Simple but for the fact that Ruth was likely to resent every minute Meghan spent there.

Luke told the girls that afternoon. ''Meghan's going to be taking care of you for a few days while I'm out of town.''

She pretended not to notice Ruth's scowl.

The following day, Meghan brought the girls home from school, along with her suitcase.

Luke kissed each girl in turn. ''I'll call every night.''

Annie tugged at Meghan's hand. ''C'mon. We got your room all ready.''

The kiss Luke planted on her cheek took her by surprise. ''Thank you,'' he said.

Meghan inspected the bedroom. It charmed her. A double-wedding-ring quilt covered the four-poster bed. An antique dressing table occupied one corner. Lace curtains let in the sunshine.

She fumbled her way through making tortillas for dinner and scorched one of Ruth's blouses while ironing it. She was batting a thousand, she congratulated herself by the end of the first day.

The second day went scarcely better, with Ruth remaining withdrawn and sullen.

Following dinner, Meghan and Annie made a game of washing and putting away the dishes. From the corner of her eye, Meghan saw Ruth watching them warily. Meghan knew Ruth resented her friendship with Annie. She wanted to join, but didn't know how.

Ruth reminded her of a spitting but lonely kitten, desperately wanting petting but afraid to let anyone close. Instead, it scares everyone away, then whimpers because it's alone. Of course, she could be reading the situation—and Ruth—entirely wrong. Her experience was limited, at best. But her instincts . . . and her heart . . . urged her to try to reach the little girl. When Annie raced off to change into her nightgown, Meghan turned to Ruth.

''I know something's bothering you. Sometimes it helps to tell someone.''

''Who? You?''

Ruth's sneer hit Meghan square in the heart, but she held to her resolve. ''Why not?''

Along with her uncle's dark eyes, Ruth also shared his ability to keep her thoughts to herself.

''I care about you,'' Meghan said, feeling her way and praying she didn't scare Ruth off.

"Why should you?" Ruth spat out. "My own mother didn't want me."

So stunned she couldn't answer, Meghan simply stared. "Why do you say that?" she asked when the silence became unbearable.

"I heard her tell Dad. That last night . . . before . . ."

Surely, Ruth had misunderstood, Meghan thought. A child didn't always pick up on the nuances, the subtleties in adult conversations. Ruth had heard something, but it couldn't be what she was saying now. *It couldn't.*

"Tell me what you think you heard," Meghan invited.

Ruth spared her a pitying glance. "I know what you're trying to do. Make me think that my mother wanted me and Annie. Well, you can't." Those too-old eyes filled with tears. "She told Dad that she wished we'd never been born. That we made it so she was stuck here in the back of beyond."

The words were a dispassionate recitation, too adult for a child to have made up. Meghan ached for Annie and Ruth and their father. As for Christine, she tried to feel some sorrow, but it wouldn't come. All she felt was revulsion for a woman who'd left such a bitter legacy for her children.

"I can't change how your mother felt," she said, picking her way carefully. "But I care about you. And so does your uncle. He loves you."

Ruth swiped at her eyes. "You'll go away. Come the end of the year, you'll be gone." Meghan felt tears pricking her own eyes. Now wasn't the time to give in to her own emotions. "I still miss Daddy," Ruth said in a whisper. "Everyone says it'll get better with time, that I'll forget. But I don't want to forget him."

"You don't have to forget him," Meghan said. "What I think people meant is it's supposed to get easier to remember him, the good times you had together."

Ruth's eyes were shiny with tears, but something more as well. Hope. "You think so?"

"I know so. That's the way it was with my mother. She died a long time ago. But I can remember her and all the fun we had together." They'd been serious for long enough, Meghan decided. "Let's go find, Annie. She's probably wondering what we're doing."

A watery smile touched Ruth's lips. "She's probably talking to a bug or something."

Meghan's lips curved as she remembered Annie doing just that the other day. The little girl had found an ant crawling along the windowsill and had started up a conversation with it. "You're probably right."

By the time they found Annie, Meghan decided everyone needed a snack. She brought out the cookie jar, stocked with Juanita's oatmeal and raisin chews.

Milk and cookies went a long way to righting the
wrongs of the world.

Ruth studied the calendar posted on the kitchen
wall. "The White Eagle Festival is coming up in a
few weeks. We always had costumes in the past.
Juanita made them, but . . ." Her shrug said it all.

"We'll make them this year," Meghan said.

"A fairy princess costume?"

"Any kind you want," she promised recklessly.

Ruth looked up. A tiny flicker of hope lighted her
eyes. "You really think we can?"

Meghan put on her most reassuring smile. The
truth was she had no idea of how to make a costume,
fairy princess or otherwise. But she wasn't about to
tell Ruth that. "Of course we can." She held out
her hand.

Shyly, Ruth slipped her hand in Meghan's. A
bond had been forged. A fragile, tenuous bond that
could snap at any time. It was up to her to make
sure it didn't.

"Me too," Annie piped up. "I want a costume."

"What do you want to be?"

Tiny brow furrowed in thought, Annie concentrated. "A white eagle."

In for a penny, in for a pound, Meghan thought.
"Sure."

"Can we do it now?"

"Don't be silly," Ruth said. "Meghan needs to
find the things to make them first. Right?"

Meghan gave a weak smile. "Right." Maybe she could find some things in the attic. Too late, she realized she'd voiced the thought aloud.

The girls insisted they start right away.

The attic proved to be a treasure trove. One trunk held an old evening gown. Sequined and beaded, it would do for a princess dress. White plumes might serve as feathers for the eagle.

She dug further. Her search yielded a bolt of white satin, a length of velvet ribbon, and a pair of impossibly small high-heeled pumps. Her excitement grew.

By the following evening, she'd managed to make a start on the princess gown, with a promise to Annie that she'd start on the eagle costume the next day. Somehow she'd find the time to finish them, Meghan promised herself.

The nightly ritual of putting Annie and Ruth to bed was a continual delight. She ran a hand over Annie's spring-yellow curls.

The small girl settled herself more firmly on Meghan's lap and tapped the book in her pudgy hands. "Read me a story." At Meghan's raised eyebrows, Annie added, "Please."

Meghan looked at the well-worn book and smiled. *Cinderella.* The familiar words comforted all three of them as she read. A thimble-size yawn alerted her that Annie was ready for bed. Ruth followed with barely a protest.

*   *   *

The storm, which had been brewing all day, took hold by midnight. The wind howled, a mournful lament that plucked at Meghan's nerves. Shutters banged against the house, clattering with each gust of wind. She made her rounds of the house, starting downstairs. The first switch she turned off plunged the kitchen into darkness. Shadows appeared where there'd been light. Familiar objects took on ominous shapes.

"Don't be a ninny," she muttered, and went to turn off the living-room light.

A creak in the floorboards caused her to jump. She was being silly. A storm was no reason to give in to a case of nerves. She was a grown woman, for heaven's sake, not a child to cower under the bed at the first crack of thunder.

As if her thoughts had summoned the deed, a clap of thunder echoed through the night.

She'd never considered the isolation of the ranch a problem before. Now every sound was a threat, every shadow a possible menace. *Some pioneer woman you'd have made.* Here, she'd been congratulating herself on caring for the children and the house. A bit of rain and thunder and she was jumping at her own shadow.

Get a grip, woman. With that pep talk, she climbed the stairs and checked on the girls. The night-light she'd left burning spilled from the bed-room doorway, a comforting sight.

"Sleep well, little angels," she whispered.

Luke finished his business in Billings earlier than he'd expected. The meeting with Dan's lawyer had gone well. Within a couple of months, the girls would be his. Though Dan had named Luke legal guardian, he wanted to safeguard his position with them by formally adopting them.

His hotel room was paid up for another night, but he decided to start home. He felt a strange kind of excitement grip him as he turned on the highway and headed west. It wasn't that he had to get back to the girls. He knew they were in good hands with Meghan.

It just felt right to be going home.

Home. The word made him feel warm inside. Home was where he wanted to be. It hadn't always been so.

Home meant Ruth and Annie. And Meghan. The last came as a shock. When had he started thinking of her in those terms? She was doing him a favor, staying with the girls. But that was all there was to it.

That settled, he pressed down on the accelerator. Home still sounded mighty good.

His knuckles whitened as he gripped the steering wheel. Fatigue made him punchy. He turned up the volume on the radio a couple of notches. Careless could get a man killed.

Puddles shimmered beneath the glare of his head-lights, splattering the undersides of his truck. Though anxious to get home, he kept the speed down, knowing the slick road made driving treacherous. A spotty rain caused him to keep the windshield wipers on low, the steady *swish-swish* a counterpoint to his jumbled thoughts.

He hadn't liked asking Meghan for her help. Being beholden to anyone—especially a woman—didn't sit well with him. Call it old-fashioned, call it male pride, he didn't like it. A man took care of his own.

Besides, he had his nieces to think about. Meghan had already found a place in their hearts. What would happen when she went away, as she eventually would, and left them? What happened then?

Something about that stuck in his craw. That honest part of him admitted that it wasn't only Annie and Ruth he was concerned about. Was he really worried about her breaking their hearts? Or was he trying to protect his own?

The house was dark when he arrived. He let himself in through the kitchen, and left his wet boots by the door. A faint cry from the girls' room had him taking the stairs two at a time. The hallway light flicked on just as he collided with something.

"Meghan?"

"Luke." Even in the muted light, he could see the smile that lit her face. "You're back early."

"Any law against that?" He regretted the words as soon as they were out. Why did this woman have the power to goad him into snapping at her when he wanted only to hold her close?

Her smile dimmed, then died. Luke felt it go out like a light in the dark.

"I thought I heard Ruth crying," she said.

Without waiting for him, she headed to the girls' bedroom.

"It's all right, sweetheart," she crooned, perched on the side of the bed. Meghan started to lift the little girl when large hands cupped her shoulders.

"Let me," he said, reaching for Ruth.

"I can manage," Meghan said coolly.

"She's my niece."

Meghan stepped out of his way and tried not to notice that her heart was breaking. Even though he'd asked for her help, Luke didn't want her there, didn't want her near his nieces.

She paused outside the door. The mellow notes of a husky voice and a guitar echoed through the night. She listened closely to catch the words:

> Don't you fret,
> Little gal of mine,
> I've got a yarn to spin,
> A story so fine . . .

Hovering in the shadows, Meghan listened, caught not so much by the words as by the husky voice singing them with such love. She longed to join them, but she dared not. Not when Luke had made it plain he had no use for her company. So she stayed where she was. Outside.

Ruth's cries had all but stopped as the lullaby continued:

> So quit your crying,
> No need to wail,
> And listen to this
> Old cowboy's tale.

A sob snagged in her throat. Tenderness, sweet and hot, welled up inside of her. The last notes of the guitar died away. Meghan moved away at the same moment.

It wouldn't do for Luke to find her listening at the door. He'd probably accuse her of spying. At the very least, he'd say she was intruding where she wasn't wanted.

She retreated to the kitchen, cleaning counters that didn't need cleaning, polishing appliances that didn't need polishing. A faint sound alerted her that she was no longer alone. She wiped her hands on a dish towel and turned.

Luke, tall and dark, stood beneath the fluorescent light.

For long moments, they simply stared at each other. Tension arced between them, as real as the storm raging outside. For an interminable span of time, all sound ceased. Thunder didn't roar, windows didn't rattle, shutters didn't bang. The uneven bump of her heart startled her.

"Did you get an earful?" Two long strides ate up the space separating them. He curled his fingers around her arm. "I know you were outside the door. Listening."

"You couldn't have heard me," she said, without thinking. A blush crept up her face as she realized what she'd revealed.

"Your perfume gave you away." Strangely, he didn't sound angry.

Encouraged, she looked up. "It's a beautiful lullaby. Did you . . . did you write it?"

He looked embarrassed. "Yeah. One night Ruth was crying, wouldn't settle down. I started singing, making it up as I went along. She quieted down. Since then . . ." He shrugged. "She likes it."

"You love her and Annie very much."

"Yeah." *And that's the only love I'll ever give.* The words, unspoken, hung like a shadow between them.

She refused to acknowledge the disappointment that washed over her. Love wasn't part of the equation with Luke MacAllister.

Luke prided himself upon being a fair man. He

owed Meghan an apology. "I'm sorry. I was out of line up there." He swallowed. Hard. "It was raining that day. . . . Storms sometimes bring it back."

"I didn't know."

"No reason you should. I just wanted you to know."

"Thank you for telling me." Her voice was stiff with hurt.

He'd done that. He knew it, was powerless to undo it. He watched her move away, telling himself to let her go. Leave awkward enough alone.

He didn't understand what happened whenever he was with the pretty schoolmarm. She was as slim as a wand, but she packed a powerful presence, managing to destroy whatever claim he had on good sense.

Like now.

He grabbed her arm. "Don't walk away from me. Folks have been walking away from me all my life."

She turned to face him. "Maybe there's a reason."

"Maybe there is." The pain in his voice tore at her heart.

"Tell me," she said.

"When I was seven, my mother said she was going to the store. She kissed me on the cheek and promised she'd bring me back some licorice. Only she never came back. Folks said later it was because she couldn't take the isolation, the winters. I always figured it was because of me." His lips twisted into something that nearly resembled a smile. "I was always into trouble, one way or the other."

Her heart ached for the child he'd been. She wanted to go back in time and find that small boy, to give him everything he'd needed, everything he'd missed. But all she could do was reach out to the man.

He turned on his heel, primed to walk away from the past, away from her.

"Luke?"

He paused.

"Don't you walk away from me. You just shared a part of yourself with me. Now I want to share something with you."

"What?"

"This."

She put everything she had into the kiss. When Luke lifted his head, he looked as bemused as she felt. Whatever had possessed her to kiss him like that?

It wasn't sympathy, though she'd felt it. It wasn't friendship, though she hoped they were friends. It was . . . She backed away from finishing the thought.

"Good night," he said.

"Good night."

* * *

Night came more quickly as October worked its way toward November. From her window, Meghan watched as the sun dipped lower in the sky, gradually disappearing behind the mountains. It had hardly been a month since she'd come to Flintrock, but already she knew that once the sun fell in the sky, the night would come quickly and the air would have a bite to it.

She loved it here. The bigness of it, the sights and scents, the knowledge that she had only to look outside her door to find deer feeding or hear an eagle scream his triumph. It was a heady feeling, one she was growing accustomed to, but hoped she'd never take for granted.

The setting sun painted the sky red over the western ridge. The colors bled into each other, red fused with purple, fuchsia into pink, orange to yellow.

Her thoughts turned to Annie and Ruth. Were they having dinner now? Or were they already finished and starting on the nighttime routine of baths and stories? She missed the girls, their laughter and chatter, even their quarrels and complaints.

Her days at the Falling Star were over. And she knew she'd left a chunk of her heart there. How long before she gave up the rest?

Those few days had been some of the happiest of her life. They made her yearn for a family of her own, someone to care for and to care about her in return . . . someone to love.

She shook off her mood and reminded herself that tonight's date with Luke was just his way of saying thank-you for staying with the girls. He'd given her no cause to think of it as anything else when he'd called last night to invite her. No cause at all.

So why were her hands damp with perspiration, her mouth dry, her heart beating a rapid tattoo within her chest? She didn't have a chance to worry over it as a rap sounded on the door.

Face flushed, Meghan opened the door. "Hi."

A bouquet of golden mums in his arms, Luke adjusted the string tie around his neck.

That she looked good enough to eat was his first thought. The second came fast upon the heels of the first: She was just a bit nervous. The idea soothed his own nerves.

The fact was that he hadn't asked a woman for a date in more months than he cared to count. He was out of practice.

Luke took her to a country western bar, where he initiated her into the intricacies of the two-step.

"I'll never get it," she complained when she missed yet another step.

"Sure you will," Luke said, turning her into a spin.

Sure that she was going to crash into a tableful of people, she held her breath, letting it out again when he spun her back to him.

"See? You did it."

She clung to him, trying to regain her balance. "What I did is almost fall into some stranger's lap."

"I had you all the time." As if to prove his point, he tightened his hold on her. The band cooperated, segueing to a slow, dreamy song about love gone wrong. He settled his hands on her waist.

Her heart, though, refused to slow its pace in time to the music. At his nearness, it raced until she was certain Luke could feel its rapid flutter.

He sang softly along with the music, his voice a husky accompaniment that sent shivers trembling through her.

The music ended, but they made no attempt to move from the dance floor. Conversations, the clink of flatware against cheap china, ebbed and flowed around them, but they remained oblivious to all but each other.

He took a deep breath. The intent in his eyes was obvious. Just as obvious was the fact that she wanted him to kiss her. Whatever else she felt for him—and there was plenty—she wanted this kiss. He confused her, frustrated her, at times even angered her, and still she wanted him to kiss her.

He touched his lips to hers, softly at first. Once. Twice. She lifted her arms to bring him closer. Reason was disregarded, logic ignored.

His lips brushed hers in a featherlight stroke that nevertheless had her trembling. She'd known a man's kisses before. So why did this one—this man—leave her so shaken? Tenderness, as sweet as the lips that had touched hers, unfurled within her.

She wanted this. It felt right, so very right. He rested his hands at her sides. When the kiss ended, she gulped for air and tried to remember her name.

When he raised his head, he appeared as moved as she.

''I think the music's over,'' she murmured when he continued to hold her.

''I think you're right.'' But the words were spoken reluctantly, as he led her back to their table.

He took her home soon after that. Outside the cottage, she waited for the kiss that didn't come. Nor did he mention the kiss they'd shared less than an hour ago.

She was left wondering if she'd imagined those few moments on the dance floor when he had held her as close as a heartbeat.

Chapter Four

By the next afternoon, everyone in town knew that Luke MacAllister had taken the pretty schoolteacher dancing. They talked about it over the meat counter in the mom-and-pop grocery store, pondered over it in Sally's Beauty Parlor and Emporium, where perms and gossip were dispensed with equal skill, and discussed it while sipping coffee in Belle's Diner.

It hummed over the phone lines and ate up the time allotted to the monthly speaker at the Garden Club. It buzzed through the meeting of the ladies' afternoon fine sewing and stitchery group and replaced the normally desultory talk inside the barber shop.

The fact that a self-confirmed bachelor like Luke

had asked a woman out was fodder for even the most closemouthed of the town residents.

Luke was aware of the gossip. He might have resented it. Might have, but didn't. Gossip was as inevitable as winter. You put up with it because you didn't have a choice. His only response to the questions that peppered him from all sides was a smile and a shrug.

He wasn't as sure about Meghan's reaction, however. Coming from a big city like she did, she might not share his complacency over the questions that were sure to be directed at her. Being a part of Flintrock now, she was considered family. And family was fair game for gossip. Meghan might not realize it, but she'd been taken in as one of the town's own.

Maybe he ought to drop by the school. Yeah. That was what he'd do. He'd warn her what to expect and assure her that it was no big deal. After all, he'd lived here all his life. He knew the ropes of small-town living. It was only right that he should let her in on some of the secrets of survival.

He was whistling as he drove to the school. He didn't bother questioning the reason for his good mood. The fact that he was about to see Meghan was nothing more than a coincidence, he assured himself.

She was cleaning the chalkboard when he arrived. Content with watching her, he slid silently into one of the pint-size desks and waited. It was no hard-ship—no hardship at all—to watch her as she worked.

Her movements were quick without being hurried, competent without a show of superefficiency. She worked with the easy grace that he'd come to as-sociate with her. Her hair, pulled back in a braid, caught the sun as she stooped and reached.

As if sensing his presence, she turned. The slow smile that bloomed on her lips was a boost to his ego. The lady was glad to see him. He unfolded his long legs from the cramped space beneath the desk, and stood.

She crossed the room until she came to a stop a few feet from him. He could smell the citrusy scent of her shampoo. He closed the remaining space sep-arating them and settled his hands on her shoulders.

Thoughts of why he'd come disappeared as he gave in to the need to touch his lips to hers.

She tasted sweet. Incredibly sweet. He deepened the kiss. When at last he pulled away, she was smiling.

"Is that how you treat all the schoolteachers?"

He tweaked a curl that had strayed to her cheek. "No. Only the beautiful ones."

She laughed. "Maybe you ought to come for the vision and hearing screening. I think you need your eyes checked."

"My eyes work just fine. You're a beautiful woman, Meghan."

She searched his face and saw only sincerity there. No man had ever called her beautiful before. Not even her father. Especially her father, she thought with a wry smile.

He'd told her often enough that all she had going for her were her family connections. Impeccable background, he'd said, would ensure that she attracted the *right* kind of man. The right kind of man meaning his kind of man—the proper credentials, the proper bank account, the proper family. And he'd been right. She had attracted that kind of man. Or, rather, her money had. In the end, she'd understood that she had been nothing more than the bait on a very attractive hook.

For a moment, she wondered if Luke was right. She shook her head in answer to her question. What was she thinking? She knew she was no beauty.

"What brings you here?" she asked briskly.

His eyes narrowed, but he went along with her change of subject. "You and me. People are talking."

"What are they saying?"

"That I asked you out."

Her lips twitched. "Sounds pretty serious."

"Oh, it is. Come evening, they'll most likely have us engaged. By morning, we'll be hitched."

Her breath hitched at the same moment. It was all

a joke, of course. But she still couldn't help the way her heartbeat picked up or the warmth that spread through her.

"What do you suggest we do?"

"Ignore it," he said. "It'll be a nine-day wonder and then something else will come along."

She wasn't worried about the gossip. Not for herself, anyway. "You don't mind?" she asked cautiously.

"No. I grew up here. I'm used to it. I just didn't want you to be upset by it."

Touched by his sensitivity, she laid a hand on his arm. "Thank you."

"You're welcome. Now that we're the hot topic, how 'bout giving 'em something else to gossip about?"

"What'd you have in mind?"

"Spend the day with me tomorrow."

"I'd like that."

"Meghan, you came." Braids flying, Ruth raced to her side the following morning.

Meghan's heart bumped against her chest at the pleasure in the little girl's eyes. They'd come a long way. She didn't delude herself into believing that all of Ruth's problems were solved, or that she herself had the answers. Still, she couldn't help the sweet warmth that spread through her.

Annie tagged behind. "Hey, wait for me." She ran the rest of the way, barreling into Meghan.

A hand at her back, Luke steadied her and scooped Annie into his arms. "Whoa, there, Pumpkin. You just about knocked Meghan over."

Annie peered at Meghan through her bangs. "Did I hurt you?"

"No, honey. You didn't hurt me."

"You girls remember what I said?" Luke asked.

"We remember," Ruth said, some of her old sullenness showing through.

Luke set Annie down to fix both girls with a steady gaze. "This isn't negotiable. You stay away from the corral. When I'm done, we'll show Meghan around. Okay?"

Ruth nodded, good humor restored. "Okay."

Annie followed her big sister. " 'Kay."

"What was that all about?" Meghan asked when the girls raced off.

"We're working with Rusty today."

"Rusty?"

"The meanest, sorriest four-legged beast you ever set eyes on," supplied George, one of Luke's old hands. He took his hat off and swiped at his forehead with the back of his sleeve. "The boss is gonna ride him today."

Meghan shivered and turned questioning eyes on Luke.

"Don't you worry none." George jammed his hat back on his head. "Luke's the best there is."

Another hand, called Tucker, led a huge red-colored horse into the corral.

"I'll be fine," Luke said for her ears only.

She hooked her legs around the railing and prepared for the show. "Hey, cowboy," she called. "Be careful."

With a cocky grin, he tipped his hat and climbed over the fence. A couple of long strides and he was at the horse's side. He grabbed the reins and pulled himself up.

One hand hooked around the reins, the other held out for balance, he made it look easy. Almost. When the horse threw him, he scrambled out of the way, narrowly missing the flying hooves. Slapping his hat against his leg, he made it out of the corral.

Meghan managed to breathe again. "You were great out there."

"I darn near got the stuffing kicked out of me," he corrected, and pulled her to him.

He smelled of the earth, and carried a good deal of it on his person. The aroma had her wrinkling her nose, but not in distaste. She was committing it to memory. It was the scent of hardworking male and something else that was Luke's alone.

The kiss was but a breath away.

"Boss, see you a minute?" George called.

Luke glared at him before turning to give Meghan a rueful smile.

"Go on," she said. "I'll be fine."

The huge horse gave a triumphant whinny. He reminded her of the red boulders that dotted the countryside.

She squinted against the sun, trying to make out the girls. They'd been playing near the house. She spotted Ruth, now helping Juanita in the garden. But where was Annie?

Her question was answered as she saw Annie slip beneath the fence and start toward Rusty.

Meghan felt her breath rush from her in a whoosh of air. For a moment, she couldn't move. Didn't dare. Her knees were shaking so hard, she'd probably topple over if she tried to budge from where she was.

She started to call out, then thought better of it. She might spook the horse. Her heart in her throat, she slid down from her perch on the fence, approaching quietly from the other side.

"Meghan, look," Annie called. "I'm going to be like Uncle Luke when I grow up."

Meghan kept her voice low. "Annie, back away slowly. No sudden moves."

As she drew closer, she heard his loud whinny. He looked smugly pleased with himself, she thought.

With a puzzled frown, Annie did as directed. When she was safely behind Meghan, Meghan gave a relieved sigh. "Now, just keep going until you reach the fence."

Meghan gave her best schoolteacher's stare. The big horse stared right back at her. Terror coated her mouth with a coppery taste. She held her ground. She might not know much about horses, but she knew enough not to show fear. Cautiously, she held out her hand. The animal sniffed it, his enormous teeth uncomfortably close.

"You're just a big show-off, aren't you?" she asked softly.

The stallion seemed to nod.

"It's no fun being cooped up, is it?"

Luke watched, afraid that if he moved, he'd startle Rusty. Or Meghan. When he'd seen Annie inside the corral, he'd started running, even while knowing he wouldn't make it. Seeing Meghan in the same danger hadn't stopped his heart from doing somersaults in his chest. He'd made sure Annie was all right before sending her to the house with Ruth.

Meghan wouldn't stand a chance if the horse decided to strike. A moment was all it would take for him to rear back and slice down with his hooves.

Luke's shoulder still bore the scar where a gelding's razor-sharp hooves had caught him before he had managed to roll out of the way. Pictures of what the stallion could do to her filled his mind, each more horrifying than the last.

George and Tucker approached from the far side. Luke motioned them to stay back.

Meghan looked up, saw him. She was backing away now, her movements slow and steady.

"That's it," he encouraged. Gut clenched into a tight knot, he watched as she cleared the corral.

When she was out of danger, he pulled her to him and held on. "What did you think you were doing?" Anger fueled his words. He managed to get them out only after assuring himself she was all right. That he was behaving irrationally didn't keep the fierceness at bay.

Her chin lifted in a gesture he'd come to recognize. "Trying to keep Annie from getting hurt."

He tried to concentrate on something—anything— but the fear that still had chills skating down his spine. He failed.

"Do you realize what could've happened?" He barely got the words out.

"Yes," she said quietly. "That's why I had to do something."

Luke winced as a shaft of guilt lanced through him. He had no call to speak to Meghan that way. She'd only been trying to help, and he'd all but thrown it back in her face. Meghan didn't deserve the harsh words he'd spoken to her. She'd been a handy target. That was all.

He stared at her, calling himself every name he

could think of. He'd snapped at her when she'd put her life on the line to save *his* niece.

Worse yet, he'd done it for the most selfish of reasons. Guilt. Guilt that *he* hadn't been the one to save Annie, that he hadn't kept her out of danger in the first place. Regret, sharp and sweet, washed over him.

His anger died as quickly as it had erupted. The heart that had lodged fast in his throat freed itself.

"Hey, I'm all right," she said when he continued to hold her. "You can let me go."

Only then did he realize that he still had her shoulders in a bone-crushing grip. He dropped his hands.

"I ain't never seen nothing like it," George said, sidling up beside them and turning a look of admiration upon Meghan. "The boss has been trying to ride that devil for a month, and you had him practically eating out of your hand." He swiped his forehead with a sweat-stained neckerchief. "Don't mind saying, ma'am, you gave us a right bad turn."

"How'd you do it?" Tucker asked.

Meghan smiled. "He's just a bully. I learned how to handle bullies my first year teaching. You just have to let them know who's boss. They fall into line pretty quickly after that."

She called a thousand-pound horse a bully? Luke shook his head. The lady was either a fool or the bravest person he'd ever met. Right now, he didn't care to speculate on which.

"Well, I'll be," Tucker said, a grin breaking through the bushy growth of his beard and revealing tobacco-stained teeth. "A bully, huh? That's one for the books."

Luke glared at Tucker and George. "Don't you two have work to do?" Temper edged his voice. Deliberately, he stopped and drew a slow breath. It steadied him.

They took themselves off, clearly reluctant to miss whatever was going to happen next.

Luke turned back to Meghan. Without stopping to question the wisdom of it, he slanted his lips over hers. Hers parted slightly beneath his, encouraging him to take the kiss a shade deeper, make it a whisper warmer.

She tasted of a cool, damp meadow fed by a mountain stream. He kissed her again, a brush of lips this time. Her response, as shy as a fawn that might make its home in that same meadow, touched something deep within him.

When he lifted his head, he saw the confusion in her eyes. How was he supposed to explain what he didn't understand himself? Seeing her that close to injury, possible death, had stolen his good sense, it seemed, along with his self-restraint.

"Thank you," he said, his voice roughened by the kiss they'd just shared. "If it hadn't been for you . . ."

"Hey. I was there."

Moved by the tenderness of the kiss, Meghan looked up at him. The gaze he settled upon her was exasperated and something else. Protective?

The idea unsettled her. Did it mean Luke was beginning to care for her? She dared not let herself think beyond that. If he cared about her, it was only because she was the town's teacher and he felt a responsibility toward her.

Her heart rejected the ruthlessly applied logic. It wanted so much more from him, so much more for him.

"Are you sure you're all right?" he asked when she continued to stare up at him.

"Yes," she said, her voice the barest whisper. "Yes," she said again, more strongly this time. "I'm fine."

"You were lucky this time. Stallions are unpredictable."

Lucky? She didn't think so. She'd given her heart to a man who had no use for it.

The day, which had begun so brightly, ended abruptly when Luke suddenly remembered a pressing errand that needed his attention. Her disappointment that their day had been cut short was all out of proportion, she lectured herself. Luke was a busy man. She didn't expect him to neglect his duties because of her. Her pep talk fell flat as she recalled his anger.

She knew him well enough to understand it was

directed at himself, rather than her. His need to protect those around him blinded him to the reality that he couldn't be everywhere at once. She knew Luke blamed himself for the near accident. And her heart ached for him because of it.

"I . . . uh . . . came to see if you're all right after . . . after what happened today."

The skepticism in her eyes made a lie out of his words, but she nodded. "Come on in."

He looked about the cottage. A hooked rug placed in front of the door welcomed visitors. Plants and pictures, pieced quilts and flowers softened the angles of the boxy room. Small touches, yet they spelled home in an indefinable way. The lady was a homemaker in the best sense of the word.

Meghan's touch was everywhere. Old narrow-necked bottles held twigs and dried flowers. The effect was at once both homey and inviting. He fingered one of the bottles, remembering the medicine his great-aunt had dispensed from similar ones.

He wondered where she'd found the bottles. She hadn't brought much with her, as he recalled, only two suitcases.

"You've made the place real homey," he said.

Her blush deepened, making her prettier than ever. She picked up one of the bottles. "I . . . uh . . . found these in the attic. I hope you don't mind."

"I imagine Aunt Ida'd be right pleased to know her things were being used."

"I've had fun decorating. I picked up the quilt at a flea market. I've never had a real home before." She said the last almost shyly, as though she were ashamed of admitting it. "But you didn't come to talk about decorating."

"I don't know why I'm here," he said in response to the not-so-subtle challenge.

The bleak expression in his eyes tore at her heart. Wordlessly, she opened her arms. He walked into them. Her arms closed around him with a fierce gentleness. He smelled of the earth and horses and leather. The aroma should have been offensive. Instead, it struck her as right. It suited the man, as surely as did the well-worn jeans, denim shirt, and leather vest he wore.

"Don't you?" He scowled at that, so she backed off. "How about some coffee while we talk?"

He smiled faintly. "Do you invite all your kids' parents—or uncles—to unburden themselves to you?"

"Only the ones who need to." She busied herself making coffee, figuring he needed the time to collect himself. "You're hurting."

His expression darkened. "I don't need your coffee. Or your sympathy."

"I'm not offering it."

"No?"

''No.''

If she and Luke were to have any kind of future together, they needed to vanquish the shadows of the past. With her heart stammering out an uneven beat, she said the words she knew could destroy the fragile understanding they'd achieved over the past couple of weeks.

''Tell me about your brother.'' He remained stubbornly silent. ''Sometimes it helps to talk it out,'' she said.

He wanted to argue, to tell her to mind her own business. Even more, though, he wanted to do exactly as she'd suggested. To talk about those last few minutes with Dan, to try to understand what had gone wrong. He hadn't talked about it with anyone.

But the habit of keeping his feelings to himself was too strong to break. And so he remained silent. And by his silence, he consigned himself to be alone.

He'd been about to open up, Meghan thought, disappointment washing over her in bitter waves. She wanted to challenge him on it, but the words melted away as she took in the closed look on his face. She was beginning to recognize the signs. He was wrestling something so dark, so painful, that he couldn't—or wouldn't—discuss it with her.

His mouth twisted in a bleak smile.

She reached out to touch his hand.

His fingers grasped hers before she could withdraw, and squeezed gently. ''Thank you.''

''For what?''

''For being there. And for not pushing.''

If only he knew how close she'd come to doing just that, he wouldn't be thanking her.

The ache in his neck, always there, intensified. He started to rub it, when her hands stilled his. Gently, she massaged the tight tendons, her fingers easing away the stress that had been building all day.

The simple gesture soothed him, but it was more than that.

The pain was gone. A quiet peace washed over him. He stared at her in wonder.

''What . . .''

''You were in pain,'' she said. The genuine concern in her voice went straight to his heart and opened it up. It was that simple. Only it wasn't simple at all. And he found himself wanting to tell her. Everything.

Luke's lips compressed into a hard line as he talked. Once started, he couldn't seem to stop. The words came in a rush as if he could erase the pain by getting them out as swiftly as possible.

His brother had mortgaged his share of the ranch to the hilt, trying to placate his wife. When Christine had demanded yet more, Dan had borrowed money from Luke. At first, Luke had gone along with it, wanting to help Dan and his family. When the demands had grown, Luke had refused.

He'd never forget the last quarrel between himself and Dan.

Dan, with a sweetly smiling Christine in tow, had come to Luke, wanting to borrow several thousand dollars to take her on a shopping trip to New York. When Luke had refused, Christine had stormed off.

Luke hadn't tried to stop her. He didn't like Christine. Hadn't liked her since Dan had married her eleven years before. She had been a nervous, spoiled woman, with a hard-edged beauty and a taste for the expensive.

Dan had followed, barely catching up to Christine before she'd slid behind the wheel of her BMW, a birthday present from Dan. Angry at not getting her own way, she was an accident waiting to happen.

The accident *had* happened, killing Dan and Christine and leaving their two daughters orphans. As their guardian, Luke took Ruth and Annie into his home and had tried hard to make it their home.

Loving them was never the problem. He had loved both of them from the time they were born. Trying to be both mother and father, trying to make up for what they'd lost and knowing he hadn't a prayer, *that* was the problem.

He hadn't spared himself in the telling, she thought. He'd laid out the facts in a dispassionate manner that was all the more wrenching for its very lack of emotion. Beneath the details, she heard the pain. Her heart ached for him, for his nieces who had lost both father and mother, for his brother, for his wife who'd chased after happiness in things rather than in her family. Unable to change what had happened, Meghan took his hand in hers. She wanted to wipe away the grief, the self-blame, the pain.

Most of all, she wanted to tell him she loved him. But now wasn't the time.

And so she listened.

"Can you remember your mother without it hurting? . . . Ruth told me," he said in answer to her unasked question. It was something he didn't like asking. He didn't want to cause her additional pain, but he needed some hope that someday he could think of Dan without the heart-wrenching ache.

Her answer came quickly. "I can remember the good times we had. I still get sad when I remember she's gone, but it's a peaceful kind of sad." Her smile included him and gave him hope. "It never goes away completely. But it does get better."

Luke tossed a bale of hay over the side of the truck, working alongside George and Tucker as they threw out feed for the cattle they'd left in a high meadow.

The work was hot and sweaty. He spared a moment to wet down his kerchief with his canteen and then wrapped it around his neck. He sighed at the blessed coolness.

The wind would dry his skin off soon enough, but the cool cloth afforded a few minutes of relief. That's all a man could ask when the temperature climbed into the high eighties. The weather took its own sweet time catching up with the calendar, he thought. And it could change without notice. Snow wasn't unheard-of in October.

He wondered what Meghan thought of Montana weather. Funny how often his thoughts turned to her lately. And what she'd done for him. She'd given him back his brother.

He was surprised to realize that he was remembering Dan without the usual pain, but with a warm feeling of nostalgia. Even a week ago, he'd have used the memories as a fresh goad for self-blame. Now he was recalling the good times for what they were, the memories no longer colored by grief and guilt. He could cherish them without beating himself up with them.

The relief he felt was staggering. He'd carried around the weight of guilt for a year. It was time to let it go.

He lifted his face to the sun.

What a bundle of contradictions Meghan was. Strength and fire, vulnerability and innocence. Shy to the point of self-effacement when it came to herself, determined, even pushy when it came to her kids. She'd fight for them, he realized. Fight and win.

He was no longer amazed by her perception. Somewhere along the way, he had come to accept the fact that she knew him better than he did himself. The knowledge, unsettling at first, now warmed him. No one—not even his father—had so fully understood him.

His feelings were no longer his own. At one time, he'd have resented that. With Meghan, though, he had accepted it, savoring the knowledge that he was not alone.

That they'd locked horns occasionally didn't lessen his admiration for her. If anything, it increased it. The lady didn't back down, nor did she compromise. Not when it came to her students. She demanded the best for them, the best from them. They were lucky to have her.

"Hey, Boss, you gonna stand around daydreaming, or you gonna help us get this feed out?" George demanded.

Caught, Luke muttered something rude. But he was grinning as he got back to work.

Luke dropped by that evening. "I wanted to thank you for last night. It's been a long time since I talked with anyone like that."

He stood so tall, so straight, broad shoulders thrown back, head tilted slightly toward her, somehow managing to look both strong and vulnerable at once.

Meghan thought he had never been quite so appealing as he was at this moment.

''The White Eagle Festival's Saturday night,'' he said. ''Will you go with me ... and Annie and Ruth?''

Words of acceptance hovered on her tongue. Yet she hesitated. She was grateful that Luke had opened up with her last night. She felt closer to him ... closer and more in love than ever.

What had made him open up? Maybe because she had shared something of herself, her vulnerability and pain. Maybe because he was learning to trust her. And maybe, just maybe, he was beginning to care.

She clung to the latter.

She'd never been any good at lying to herself, and she didn't try now. What was the point? She was in love with Luke MacAllister. Pretending that all she felt for him was friendship was the ultimate in self-deception. Falling in love with him was probably one of the most foolish things she'd ever done.

Acknowledging her love didn't change the situation, though. Luke had made it plain from the beginning that he wasn't looking for a relationship. He liked her, but that was all he would allow himself to feel for her.

She had no right to complain. She'd known the rules. That she'd gone and broken them was no one's fault but her own. She feared spending an evening with him would only deepen her feelings. Was it really worth the added pain?

Luke caught her hand. "I know we've got things to work out. But I'd like for us to have this night. Together."

"All right."

The pleasure in his eyes warmed her. His fingers closed around hers.

The reminder of that moment gave her courage as she dressed for the festival a few days later. She chose a full denim skirt and a western-style blouse. Butter-soft leather boots completed the look.

When Luke arrived to pick her up, her heart turned over as she registered his masculine appeal. A white shirt drew attention to the breadth of his shoulders, the deep tan of his face. Black jeans with a turquoise-studded belt were his concession to dressing up.

He escorted her to the truck. "Sorry about that. Juanita needed the car."

"No problem," she said.

The seat looked far from the ground. She started to hitch up her skirt when strong arms lifted and scooted her inside before she could protest.

"Out here, we know how to treat a lady," was the only explanation he made.

She was grateful for Annie and Ruth's chatter, which filled the silence.

Booths lined the fairgrounds. Tempting aromas spilled from the chuck wagon set up in the center of the ring. Smoke from hamburgers and hot dogs cooking on a grill thickened the air. The spicy scent of fried onions had her stomach rumbling. She flattened a hand against it, remembering she'd skipped lunch to finish the girls' costumes.

Holding hands with Luke and Meghan, Annie chattered happily. "See, Uncle Luke? Feathers." She pointed to the white plumes decorating her hair.

"I see." His gaze found Meghan's before settling on his niece. "You'll be the cutest eaglet in the festival."

"What's eag . . . eaglet?"

"A baby eagle."

Annie flapped around in a flurry of fluttering plumes. "I'm flying." She came to rest by Meghan's side, her hand stealing into Meghan's. The gesture was so sweet and trusting that Meghan blinked back tears.

Her eyes sought Luke's. The warm approval she read there caused her to tighten her hold on Annie's hand.

"Ouch," Annie said, tugging her hand away. "You're squeezing. Hard."

"I'm sorry," Meghan said, her eyes still on Luke. "I didn't mean to hurt you."

"It's all right." Annie slipped her hand back into

Meghan's. "You were probably thinking about Uncle Luke."

Meghan felt the color steal into her cheeks.

"Uncle Luke?"

"What, Pumpkin?"

"You like Meghan, don't you?"

"Yeah," he answered, his eyes never leaving Meghan's. "I like her."

"So do I." Annie pulled at Meghan's hand. "Do you like Uncle Luke?"

Meghan felt her cheeks grow warm. "Of course I do."

"Why don't you marry him? Then you could be my mommy. And Ruth's."

Her blush grew brighter. She looked to Luke for help. To her chagrin, he only grinned, amusement dancing in his eyes. *How are you going to get out of this?* he asked, without saying a word.

"How do I look, Uncle Luke?" Ruth asked shyly, sparing Meghan the need to answer Annie.

Luke turned to regard his older niece with serious eyes. "Like a princess. A beautiful princess." He kissed her cheek.

Meghan watched as pleasure brightened Ruth's pale cheeks. Somehow he'd known that Ruth, hovering between childhood and the teen years, needed those exact words.

She threw her arms around her uncle's neck. "Thanks. I'm going to show my friends." She hesitated before hugging Meghan. "Thanks for . . . you know."

"What was that all about?" Luke asked after Ruth took off.

"Girl stuff," she said.

"I have a feeling there's a lot of girl stuff going on around here lately."

Annie started to follow her older sister.

"Hey, Pumpkin, where do you think you're going?"

"To show my costume to my friends. Can I, Uncle Luke? Can I? Please?" Annie smiled her uncle's slow smile, the one guaranteed to charm birds from the trees.

Meghan's heart gave a hop, skip, and jump.

"I'll be right back," Annie said. "Promise."

"Okay."

"They'll be fine," Meghan said.

"With everything that's been going on, I forgot all about the costumes. Ruth said you made them?"

She nodded.

"It seems I have a lot to thank you for." His smile, a masculine version of Annie's, warmed her through and through.

Hattie Paige bustled over to them. "Glad to see you two made it tonight." She fixed Luke with a stern look. "Why aren't you asking Meghan for a dance?"

"I was just about to," he said, his eyes on

Meghan. "Dance with me . . . please." His hand fitted to the small of her back, he guided her to the
dance floor.

The band played a slow, dreamy song of love
gone wrong. The plaintive words tugged at her heart-
strings. Other dancers milled around them, but she
was oblivious to all but the man who held her.

When the music segued into a lively tune, she
knew a sharp sense of regret as Luke loosened his
hold and swung her around. A square dance followed, and she found herself passed from partner to
partner as she moved through the sequences of the
reel.

Breathless at the end of the dance, she made her
way to the refreshment table and reached for a cup
of punch.

"I thought I'd never get near you again," Luke
said, coming up behind her and settling his hands on
her waist. He turned her to him.

At that moment, Annie wedged between them.
"Uncle Luke, Meghan. It's time to break the
piñata."

He exchanged a rueful look with Meghan, his eyes
promising that there'd be another time.

A piñata in the shape of a donkey was suspended
from a pole. Children lined up. Meghan handed the
first child a plastic bat. The small boy took a swing
at the piñata.

"Good try," she said when his swat failed to break it.

"Next."

The next few kids managed to dent it, but the crepe paper and wire structure held fast.

Ruth stepped up. "Watch, Uncle Luke." She swung at the piñata, whacking it soundly. Candy, glistening like jewels in foil wrapping, spilled from the donkey.

Luke hooked an arm around Meghan's waist, drawing her to him.

There, beneath the twinkling colored lights, the cheers and squeals of excited children now but a distant background noise, Luke kissed her. She gave herself up to the sweetness she found in his lips.

It was a perfect moment, one she wished would last forever.

Reality intruded in the form of two sleepy children.

After he'd dropped the girls off at the ranch, Luke took her home. He'd said nothing more about the kiss they'd shared, and she was grateful. It had been a kiss to curl her toes, and she wanted time to savor it for a time before she talked about it.

Besides, what was there to say?

It was only a kiss. Sure, it was the most devastating kiss she'd ever experienced, but she couldn't read any more into it than that.

She had to remember her relationship with Luke

was destined to remain a friendship. She'd reminded herself often enough that he had no intention of marrying. Ever.

But she also knew that what she felt for him went far beyond mere friendship. The sense of deep recognition that she experienced whenever she was with him continued to startle her. He touched something inside of her that had remained dormant up until now. If only Luke would let himself *feel*. . . .

Her thoughts returned, as she'd known they would, to the kiss. It had been a kiss to steal a woman's breath and make her forget all she'd ever learned about guarding her heart. She feared it was too late. She'd already given her heart. And to a man who'd made it clear that he didn't believe in love.

She kept her distance, because she sensed he wanted it that way. Someday, she promised herself, someday, she'd close that distance. For now, she was content with what they had.

She pressed her palm to his cheek before settling her lips on his.

He looked surprised, but not displeased. "What was that for?"

"Because," she said. "Just because." She left him to wonder over that as he let himself out.

Chapter Five

The colors had deepened as autumn edged closer to winter. The sun still burned brightly, but the days had grown shorter, the nights longer. Deer foraged closer to town, looking for food, Luke had told her. One day she'd even managed to get close enough to snap a picture of a doe and her fawn.

With each day that passed, she knew she was adding another link to the chain that kept her there. An invisible chain, one forged with traditions both large and small, and, most of all, love.

Flintrock felt like home. No, that wasn't right. It didn't just feel like home; it *was* home. Her home. For the first time since her mother had died, she had a home.

The knowledge sent a rush of joy singing through

her. She'd known pleasure, even happiness, but this feeling of pure joy was new.

A home. Never mind that it was a cottage, a far cry from the mansion where she'd grown up. Bits and pieces of things she'd collected cluttered the surfaces of tables and bookcases. Dust even clung to a few of them. The thought had her lips kicking up at the corners. Dust hadn't been allowed in the house she'd called home for most of her life. Now she viewed it as a symbol, a badge of her independence.

No, her home wasn't perfect in a pristine sense. Perfection, she'd decided, was boring. And stifling. But it was hers. And all she needed.

The last gave her pause. Was it all she needed? What about a husband, children? Her mind conjured up a picture of Luke and his nieces. A home needed a family. *She* needed a family.

When Luke arrived to take her to dinner Friday evening, she couldn't suppress a tiny flare of hope that he might be coming around to accepting that he had feelings for her.

They kept the conversation light, touching on the festival, the children's schoolwork, the upcoming Thanksgiving pageant.

"How did you get into costume-making?" he asked over coffee and dessert.

Meghan opened her mouth to tell him that she'd never made a costume before in her life. And closed it without speaking. The hostess was just leading a man in from the bar. A man whose hand-tailored suit set him apart from the restaurant's other patrons. Her father.

"Meghan."

The sound of her name delivered in those sonorous tones still had the power to cause her to flinch.

"Father."

She had never addressed Chandler Sullivan as anything less than the formal "father." No dad, or pop, or even daddy for him. He was *FATHER*. She had always thought of him in capital letters. She knew he expected no less.

"I was told you might be here."

"You were?"

She remembered her manners enough to make the introductions.

Chandler Sullivan acknowledged Luke's presence with a curt nod of his head before turning his attention back to Meghan.

Luke started to excuse himself, but Meghan laid a hand on his arm. "Stay. Please."

With a glance at her father and then at her, he sat back down. He angled his chair closer to hers and reached for her hand beneath the table. The quick squeeze warmed her as nothing else could.

While the men sized each other up, Meghan took the opportunity to compare them. Both carried themselves with a cool confidence. Both had strong, good looks, although her father's were those of a man now past his prime. Yet for all their similarities, Meghan sensed an essential difference in the two men.

Luke radiated a quiet authority that came from within. If he were to lose everything, he'd still retain the same determination and purpose. Her father's authority stemmed from the trappings of outward success—money and influence. Take those away, and he would be nothing. The thought filled her with power.

"I've talked with Trenton," Chandler said to Meghan, apparently dismissing Luke as not worthy of his attention. "He's understandably upset by your behavior."

She barely repressed an unladylike snort.

Her father's lips tightened, but he gave no other sign he'd noticed her reaction. "He's willing to take you back."

"Under the circumstances, that's very generous of him." Sarcasm, which she made no attempt to disguise, coated her words. "No."

Chandler's eyebrows rose in silent inquiry.

"Tell Trent thanks, but no thanks."

"Trenton Ross is one of the most eligible bachelors in the northwest. You can't afford to dismiss him for such a flimsy reason."

"I don't consider finding out that my fiancé cheated on me a flimsy reason."

"A misunderstanding."

Meghan studied the man seated across the table

from her and realized he'd never understood her . . . or even tried to.

"Is that all you had to say?" she asked.

He donned what she had privately termed his I-know-best-and-you'd-better-listen mantle. "I wasn't going to say anything, but Trenton let it drop that if you came back, he'd entertain the idea of merging our two businesses. I don't have to tell you what that would do for Sullivan Enterprises."

"Thank goodness," she murmured.

"What was that?"

"That you don't have to tell me."

Luke gave a chuckle quickly disguised as a cough. The slight pressure on her fingers encouraged her to face her father's disapproval.

His lips compressed into a hard line. "Living out in the back of beyond has given you an odd sense of humor. Where is your family loyalty?" He didn't give her time to answer. "Sullivan Enterprises could use an influx of cash. The industry is suffering some setbacks."

She knew business was all-consuming with her father, but she hadn't expected that even he would stoop so far as to barter his only child. "Is that what this is all about? You want to use me as some kind of bargaining chip?" She couldn't quite keep the horror from her voice.

"Certainly not. But it wouldn't hurt to consider the long-term ramifications."

"The long-term ramifications are that I'd be tied to a man I don't love and who doesn't love me."

"Love." He spat the word. Fascinated, she watched as his face underwent some kind of transformation. Something approaching a smile curled his lips. "You know how much you mean to me."

"I know exactly how much I mean to you." Tears warmed the back of her eyes, but she kept them in check.

The parody of a smile vanished from her father's face. "Never mind that I have only your best interests at heart." He said the words stiffly, a litany delivered so often that he no longer had to think about it, Meghan thought resentfully.

That Chandler Sullivan had never had any interests at heart but his own was a truth Meghan chose to keep to herself. To give voice to it would only bring on a lecture on the duties of a grateful child toward a benevolent parent, a lecture she was loath to hear again.

She thought back to the days and weeks after her mother had died and remembered the misery that had enveloped her and the loneliness that had accompanied it. Tentatively, she'd reached out to her father. They'd never been close before, but surely, she'd thought, they could find some kind of common ground, if not affection, then respect.

She'd been wrong. He had brushed her off as he would an annoying insect. Still, she'd tried. She'd excelled in school, earned half a dozen scholarships, and won scores of awards, all in an attempt to make him proud of her. Her efforts had met with the bland assumption that he expected no less.

Every day she'd hoped, prayed, for a token of love, a scrap of affection, the chant as familiar to her as her own heartbeat. Her prayers had gone unanswered until even her childish persistence had given up.

She'd longed for his acceptance, if not his love, for as long as she could remember. She had seen that need as weakness, but now she wondered if maybe it wasn't so much weak as it was human.

It had taken twenty-six years for her to understand and accept the truth. Her father didn't love her. Had never loved her. She doubted he had it in him to love anyone. Ever. Whatever passion he felt was reserved for his business and his social standing.

The knowledge was freeing. After a lifetime of trying to gain his approval, if not his love, she could accept now that nothing—no accomplishment, no award, no honor—could achieve that. It was simple, really. He couldn't give what he didn't have.

She looked up at the man who had given her life and then ignored her when she'd failed to be the son he'd wanted. "Good-bye, Father."

He brushed an imaginary fleck of dust from his jacket and then left without a word.

Meghan watched him walk away. Blindly, she turned to Luke.

He threw some bills on the table, gathered up her wrap and purse, and led her outside. Once in the truck, he gathered her to him. The tears came then. Quiet, gentle tears that were somehow more devastating than noisy, wrenching sobs.

He closed his arms around her and rocked her back and forth.

After long moments had passed, she pulled away and swiped at her eyes. ''I'm sorry,'' she whispered, dredging up ingrained manners and a fragile smile.

''Don't be.'' Luke handed her his handkerchief. ''Blow.''

She did so and then hiccuped. ''He didn't want a marriage for me, but a merger for his business. His business.'' She all but shouted the last word.

Luke took her in his arms again and held on. She felt small and soft and vulnerable.

''Thank you,'' she said at last, managing a watery smile. ''Just what you wanted on our date—a blubbering female.''

''You didn't blubber,'' he said. ''And I didn't do anything to deserve your thanks.''

''You were there.''

He didn't want her reading anything into his actions. The fact was, he didn't want to look at those actions too closely himself. Meghan had needed someone, and he was handy. End of story. He didn't

like to see anyone hurting. It was no big deal. Anyone would have done the same thing. He said as
much, only to have her shake her head.

"Not anyone," she said. "Just like not anyone
would have taken in his nieces when their parents
died."

He wanted to argue. She was making him out to
be some kind of knight on a white horse. Nothing
could be further from the truth. Meghan continued
to stare up at him with such warmth in her eyes that
he squirmed inwardly.

No other woman had ever had such an effect on
him. He could almost imagine that he had a chance
at a future with Meghan.

He reminded himself that she was hurting. She
needed a friend. With that in mind, he patted her
shoulder and tried to ignore the hurt in her eyes
when he pulled away.

Meghan didn't need to be a mind reader to understand why Luke had pulled away. No man wanted
a watering pot for a date. She'd promised herself that
they'd keep things light. Instead, she'd cried on his
shoulder and turned what should have been a casual
dinner into something out of a soap opera.

He took her home after that. A quick kiss to her
cheek, a promise to call tomorrow, and he was gone.

Well, she couldn't blame him. The man had been
forced to witness the scene between her father and

her and then she'd cried all over him like some hysterical female. Why should he want to stick around for the next act?

Her philosophical attitude was all well and good, but it didn't block out the pain. Accepting that her father didn't love her hurt more than she'd anticipated. For a moment she wondered if she would have been better off not knowing the truth.

Slowly, she shook her head. Deep down, in that place where lies are rejected and only the truth can survive, she'd already known. Tonight had only confirmed what she'd been afraid to admit.

Her father didn't love her. So what? Lots of people faced worse tragedies than that every day. She wasn't the first child to be rejected by a parent; she wouldn't be the last. Her chin firmed. She wasn't about to indulge in some pity party. She had a new life, a new job, new friends. Whatever Chandler Sullivan felt or didn't feel, she would make it. On her own.

The words felt good.

Luke hadn't trusted himself last night to confront Meghan's father. Today he hunted up Chandler Sullivan. Finding him wasn't hard. Flintrock boasted only one hotel. He caught Sullivan just as he was checking out.

"Sullivan. I want to talk with you."

Meghan's father gave him a hard stare. "The boy-friend. Right?"

"A friend."

"I'm in a hurry."

Luke laid a hand on the older man's arm, stopping his progress.

Sullivan turned on him, his lips pulled back in a snarl. "Okay. You want to talk, talk."

Luke gestured to a sofa in the lobby, somewhat secluded by potted plants. He waited until they were both seated before saying, "Meghan's hurting. She needs to know you love her." When Sullivan remained silent, Luke grabbed him by the shirt. "She's your daughter, man."

"I don't have a daughter." Whatever Luke had hoped for, it wasn't the cold words delivered in an equally cold tone.

"You don't know what you have in Meghan."

"An ungrateful child who continues to disappoint me."

Luke kept a rein on his temper. "Have you ever asked her what she wants, what she feels, what she dreams?"

"I arranged an advantageous marriage for her, not easy when you consider her lack of looks. What else does she expect of me?"

Luke ignored the reference to Meghan's looks and focused on what was important. "Maybe a little love."

''Love doesn't pay the bills.'' Sullivan stood, legs braced, a powerful bulldog of a man with cold eyes and, it seemed, an even colder heart.

Luke got to his feet as well. He wanted to ram his fist in Sullivan's gut. Only concern for Meghan kept his hands at his sides. She wouldn't appreciate his interference on her behalf. ''Is that all your daughter is to you? A business asset?''

Sullivan pushed past Luke. ''Tell my daughter she knows where to find me if she changes her mind.''

Luke watched as the old man walked away, his angry strides eating up the short distance to the door.

''Mr. Personality leave?'' Hattie Paige asked, crossing the room to stand by his side.

''Yeah.''

''Good riddance.''

Luke gave her a curious look. As far as he knew, Hattie didn't even know the man, much less have a reason to dislike him.

''I was there last night when he tore into Meghan,'' she said, apparently reading his mind. ''If someone wants to run a spit through the man and barbecue him over an open flame, I'll bring the potato salad.'' She took a deep breath. ''It fairly makes my blood boil, the way he treated her. That girl's been good for the kids, good for the town.''

Luke patted her arm. ''I don't think he'll be coming back.''

"Meghan's got a family here," Hattie said. "We take care of our own."

Not for the first time, Luke was grateful for his hometown. It wasn't perfect. It had its share of problems—namely, neighbors who knew more about your business than you did and didn't mind telling you how you ought to be minding it. But it took care of its own. Whether Meghan knew it or not, she'd been accepted. And, because of that, she was family.

Maybe he ought to share that with her.

He found her at the edge of the small garden plot that bordered the cottage. In jeans and a pink shirt, with her hair pulled into twin braids, she didn't look much older than Ruth.

She was digging up the ground, attacking the dirt with nothing more than a spade and vengeance. He watched as she then set each bulb in place, the gentleness of her hands in contrast with her earlier assault.

She was pale, but composed. He admired that. The lady had pride and more than her share of guts. Well, he wouldn't add to her misery by recounting the scene with her father. From what he'd seen, she was better off without Chandler Sullivan.

"You look like you know what you're doing," he said.

He was rewarded by the faint color in her cheeks. "I always wanted to have a garden . . . to plant roots."

He knew she was talking about more than simply growing flowers. "This is your first one?" He offered her a hand up.

She grimaced as she stood. "The first one I get to take care of myself."

He didn't have a chance to ask her what she meant by that.

"I'm sorry about last night," she said.

"What for?"

Her smile was tinged with exasperation. "Come on, Luke. When you asked me out, you didn't bargain for a family fight in the middle of the town's one hotel."

"Neither did you."

"No," she said. "I didn't."

"Your father's a fool." He'd wager that not many people called Chandler Sullivan a fool. From what Luke had seen of the man, he was accustomed to getting his own way.

"My father usually gets what he wants," she said, echoing his own thoughts.

"But not this time?"

Her chin lifted. "Not this time."

"That-a girl." He paused and studied her, wondering how much he dared ask, how much he had the *right* to ask. "Tell me about this fiancé of yours."

"What do you want to know?"

"His name'll do for starters."

"Trenton Ross II."

"Trenton Ross II. Sounds like some kind of pedigreed poodle."

That earned a smile from her. "Trent knew how to sweep a woman off her feet. Candlelight dinners. Flowers. Gifts for no occasion. When he asked me to marry him, I said yes." It hurt to remember how naive she'd been, how foolish to believe a man with movie-star looks like his had wanted her.

"Did you love him?"

"I wanted to believe I did." She'd been in love with the idea of being in love. And getting away from her father. The knowledge shamed her. She'd been willing to marry a man she didn't love for no better reason than cowardice. "Trent was the perfect man for me. Everyone said so."

"Including your father?"

"Especially my father. He said Trent was the son he'd always wanted."

"What made Trent so great?"

"He was *right*."

"Right?"

"He had the right look, the right background, the right job. Everything about him was right." She spat out the last word. "Everything but the fact that he was cheating on me all the time we were supposed to be engaged. When I found out what was going on, I confronted him. You know what he did? He laughed. Said I knew what was going on when I agreed to marry him."

"What happened then?"

"I told him it was off. I gave him back his ring." She remembered the humiliation of canceling arrangements, returning gifts, making explanations to friends and family. She hadn't known then that that would be the easy part. Telling her father that she'd broken the engagement had been far more difficult.

"My father said I was lucky Trent gave me a second look. That a woman like me couldn't expect to land someone like Trent without giving up a few things." She hadn't understood her father's anger. Not then. Not until his visit had she realized the extent of his scheming.

She stopped, waiting for some kind of reaction. When Luke kept quiet, she continued. "He told me that Trent was a good match and that I ought to be happy he was still willing to have me."

"What did you do?"

"I got my own place. Pretty pathetic, huh? A twenty-six-year-old woman still living at home. I was working at a private school when I saw your ad." She shrugged. "You know the rest."

"You mean the part about you leaving everything you'd ever known to come to a town so small it doesn't even have its own post office to be a teacher to thirty-six kids of all different ages?" He hadn't fully appreciated before how much courage that must have demanded, how much of herself she'd had to leave behind.

Her smile was lopsided. ''Yeah. That part.''

''You know, you have a lot of friends here. And I don't mean just the children. You're part of the family.''

''Family?''

''The town.''

''I like that. I like that a lot.''

''Don't be too sure,'' he warned, playful now. ''Being part of the town family means everyone has the right to butt in to your life. If you change the way you wear your hair, someone'll feel bound to tell you they liked it better the way you had it. Like me. I like your hair just fine.''

''Do you?''

''Oh, yeah.''

''It's a mess.'' She swiped at a stray piece with a grubby hand, streaking her cheek with the dark soil.

''Let me.'' Gently, he dabbed at the smudge and only succeeded in smearing it more.

''My turn.'' She daubed some dirt on his cheeks.

Of course, he had to retaliate. By the time they were finished, they were covered with dirt and giggling like children. The sound of Meghan's laughter filled him with satisfaction.

He wasn't egotistical enough to believe that he'd solved her problems with her father. But if he'd managed to lighten her mood, even for a few minutes, it was enough.

The patchy sunlight scattered through her hair.

Without thinking, he twirled a finger through a curl and settled a hand at the small of her back, urging her closer until they were but a heartbeat apart. He touched his lips to hers.

He'd meant the kiss to be no more than a brush of lips, a bit of comfort. To please himself, to please them both, he deepened it until he could scarcely breathe, much less think straight.

She smiled up at him. For a moment, he wondered if he'd imagined what had just taken place between them. She appeared untouched by the kiss they'd just shared. Until he looked at her eyes and saw the brightness that burned beneath the deep brown. He could see the pulse that fluttered at the base of her throat, hear the ragged breathing that she was struggling to disguise.

Meghan put her hands to his chest and pushed gently. "I'd better get cleaned up." She started toward the house, turned, paused. "Thank you."

He didn't pretend to misunderstand. "You're welcome." He turned on the hose. "I'll wash up out here . . . if you don't mind."

She shook her head. "I don't mind."

There was a lot about Luke MacAllister that she didn't mind, she thought as she cleaned up. There was a lot about him to admire. His kiss had turned her world upside down.

She'd come to Flintrock to start a new job . . . a new life. She hadn't come looking for love. But she had a feeling that it had found her.

Chapter Six

Juanita had promised Meghan a cooking lesson in making tortillas.

Meghan straddled a stool, watching as Juanita deftly shaped the dough into balls. "You've been with Luke for a long time?"

"Since he was a boy." Juanita poured some oil into a frying pan. "He was always asking questions, wanting to know why."

Meghan smiled. She could believe that. A man like Luke would always want to know why things were the way they were. When they didn't fit his ideals, he'd work to change them.

It was but one of the reasons she loved him. Now she wondered if that same obstinacy would work against her. He didn't believe in love. Trying to convince him that she loved him wouldn't be easy.

117

Juanita rolled out the dough into rough circles. Satisfied, she looked up from her task. "You like him. Yes?"

"I like him. Yes."

Juanita pronounced the oil ready. She fried the first tortilla, sliding it into the pan with scarcely a ripple. "Your turn."

Meghan flipped the second tortilla into the pan, managing to tear the edges.

"You must ease it into the pan," Juanita said.

When Meghan removed it, she grimaced at the burnt edges.

"We will try again."

By the time they finished, Meghan had two perfect tortillas to show for her efforts, and a dozen or so burnt ones.

Juanita filled the sink with soapy water and then gestured to Meghan. "Part of cooking is cleaning up."

Meghan dipped her hands in the sudsy water, enjoying the simple task of washing the dishes.

Juanita dried the dishes and put them away. "Mr. Luke is a good man. A strong man. He needs a strong woman to love him." She eyed Meghan with knowing eyes. "You are strong."

Meghan had never thought of herself as strong. For too long, she'd allowed others to rule her life. But no longer. "You're right. I *am* strong."

A wide grin split Juanita's face. "You are good for him. And the little ones."

"I want to be," Meghan whispered.

"You're very young. You're also beautiful and intelligent." She held up a hand when Meghan would have protested. "Having a man in your life doesn't diminish those things. The right man . . ." Her smile came then. "The right man enhances them."

"Luke doesn't need me." The words burned her throat, but she got them out.

Juanita's expression gentled. "Luke doesn't give his trust easily. He doesn't want to need you. But he does. And that's what he's fighting. Not you. But himself. It's up to you to show him what he's missing."

How was she supposed to show Luke MacAllister anything, Meghan wondered. He didn't want anyone in his life. Anyone except Ruth and Annie, that is. She said as much.

Juanita patted Meghan's hand. "When the time comes, you'll know what to do."

He needs you. The words played over and over in her mind. Did he? Or were they the product of an overactive imagination of a romantic old lady?

"Follow your heart. It won't lead you astray."

The words drew a faint frown from Meghan. She'd never trusted her heart before, never dared to.

Now she was being challenged to not only trust it but to follow it. Did she have the courage?

Luke drove to Meghan's cottage, anger propelling him on. Meghan had no right involving Juanita in their relationship. He replayed the conversation he'd just had with his housekeeper, his lips tightening.

"I have seen you together," Juanita had said. "She is your heartsong."

He wasn't ready to hear that, wasn't sure he'd ever be ready. With a curt order to Juanita to mind her own business, he'd taken off. He rapped on the cottage door, scarcely giving Meghan time to open it before he burst inside.

"Luke, is something—"

"Juanita's got some notion that you and I belong together."

The color sprang to her cheeks. "She doesn't mean anything. She just cares about you, about the girls. She wants to see you happy."

"And you're the one who can do that?" The sneer in his voice had her hackles rising. "I don't think so. Just because we shared a few kisses—"

"Why don't you admit that you wanted to kiss me as much as I wanted to kiss you? Or are you scared?"

Challenge singed the air. She didn't give him a chance to rise to it, but poked him in the chest with her finger.

"Here's a news flash for you, Mr. MacAllister. You aren't the great catch you seem to think you are. You're arrogant and pigheaded and you've got an ego the size of Montana." She jabbed him with each word. "What makes you think I'd want you? All I see is a cowboy with more conceit than brains."

He said the only thing he could. "I'm sorry."

He'd been an arrogant jerk. Moreover, he knew it. The fact was, he was running scared, just as Meghan had said.

"Yeah? Well, so am I." She held the door open. "Don't let it hit you in the backside on the way out."

He took the hint, not at all certain she wouldn't slam the door on him on his way out. A reluctant grin played about his lips. Darn, if the pretty lady hadn't given him what for. He didn't much like what she'd had to say, but he liked how she'd said it. Courage and fire. The lady had both. In spades.

She'd let him have it with both barrels. Her words buzzed through his mind, like angry bees in a hive, stinging him with their truth. For she had spoken the truth. He *was* afraid. Afraid that he might care. Caring led to love. And love made a man vulnerable.

A smart man would stay away. A smart man would cut his losses while he still had the chance. A smart man would do a lot of things.

Luke had always thought of himself as a smart man. But not this time.

He waited until school was out the following day and caught Meghan just as she was leaving. He held out a peace offering. "An apple for the teacher."

Without a hint of a smile, she took it, placed it on a stack of books, and started toward the door.

"Can I carry your books for you?" he asked. Without waiting for her consent, he took the books from her and tucked them beneath his arm.

The smile he'd hoped to see tilted the corner of her mouth, but she quickly wiped it away. "If you're coming, let's go. I've got papers to grade."

He matched his pace to hers. "About yesterday . . ."

"What about yesterday?"

"I was a jerk."

She spared him a glance, but kept right on walking. "You got that right."

"Are you gonna forgive me?"

"That depends."

"Oh what?"

"On whether you're going to keep on acting like a jerk."

He pulled her to him with his free hand. "I don't know what's happening between us. I just know I can't let you go."

I love you. He held the words deep within his heart, afraid to give them away.

I love you. Meghan read the truth in his eyes, but he kept his silence. She held on to what she saw, for it was all she had.

Luke's hands settled on her shoulders. Gently, so very gently, he brushed his lips against her hair. They drifted down to her forehead before coming to rest upon her mouth.

Her lips opened to welcome his. The kiss didn't just ask; it demanded. So much so that she was overwhelmed with the need she felt within him. But there was giving as well, generous and warm and loving.

It was that to which she responded. That and the fear she sensed he kept well hidden beneath his tough-guy image. She still hadn't identified the source of that fear. But she would, she promised herself. She would.

''Is it enough to tell you that there's never been another woman as important to me as you are?'' he asked.

''It's enough,'' she said quietly. For now.

A flicker of hope overlapped her doubts. She held onto it for all she was worth. It was all she had.

Luke didn't come around for several days. She told herself he needed time. In the meantime, she had plenty to keep her busy. The children were planning a Thanksgiving pageant, complete with Pilgrims, Indians, and a feast. Her evenings were spent cutting out construction-paper hats and collars.

She should have been content, but a strange restlessness filled her, no matter how busy her days, no matter how much she crowded into her nights. She recognized the cause of her agitation. Tension. The tension of keeping her feelings to herself.

When Luke showed up one evening, she made up her mind. "I love you." The words came as easily as a breath, as softly as a sigh. "You don't have to say anything. In fact, I'd prefer you didn't. Not yet."

His eyes narrowed, but he did as she asked.

"Love's a gift," she said gently. "It doesn't ask anything in return. Except, maybe, that you accept it for what it is." She flattened her palm against his cheek, letting it linger.

She'd laid her cards on the table. The next step was his.

For the first time in days, she felt at ease. She had told Luke she loved him. She had no regrets. The tension that had been building within her had come from fighting her own feelings and hiding the truth . . . from both of them.

She'd meant what she'd said. Her love was a gift, freely given, no strings attached.

After he left, Luke touched his cheek, still warm, he imagined, from Meghan's touch. He couldn't get Meghan's declaration out of his mind.

She'd claimed that she loved him. Heaven help him, he believed her. He *wanted* to believe her. He wanted it all.

What did he know about loving? He knew what

it *wasn't*. But that didn't mean he had any idea of what it was. Was it the feeling of rightness he experienced whenever he was with her? Or the warmth that settled over him when he held her close? Or maybe it was simply knowing she was the other half of himself.

But what did he have to offer a woman?

A woman as beautiful and sensitive as Meghan could have any man she wanted. What could she want with him? A man who had more liabilities than assets. A man who came with a ready-made family and a truckload of debts.

It was far more fundamental than that, though. It had to do with the ability to love, or more exactly, the lack of that ability.

It would be so easy to believe her. To surrender to the feelings she evoked within him. He wanted it . . . his heart wanted it. But his mind was more difficult to convince. It had carefully catalogued bitter memories.

MacAllister men had a poor track record with women. Hadn't he learned anything from his father, his brother?

He reviewed the facts. He cared about her. He couldn't look at her without wanting her. He was afraid, very much afraid, that she was everything that had been missing in his life. And if she were, a tiny voice questioned, what then?

Chapter Seven

Things started to change after that. Meghan hardly dared believe the happiness that colored her days and turned the nights to magic. No, that wasn't right. Magic was too tame a word for what she was feeling.

The air grew crisper, a hint of the winter yet to come cooling the evenings. Still, autumn wore its beauty with pride. The trees were a paint box of color, emerald and primrose, scarlet and amber.

Luke had taken to spending the evenings with her, more often than not bringing Ruth and Annie with him. His smile came more often, his laughter a frequent punctuation to their time together. The girls blossomed under their combined love. Meghan started to think that every dream she'd ever dreamed, every wish she'd ever wished, was about to be fulfilled.

Through it all, there was Luke. Sometimes serious, occasionally laughing, but always loving.

She knew he was worried about how his nieces were going to handle their father's birthday, coming up in a few days.

"Annie'll probably do all right. It's Ruth I'm worried about. She and Dan were like this." He held up two fingers twisted together.

"You'll do the right thing," Meghan said.

"If I knew what it was."

Saturday, she drove to the ranch. She found Luke and the girls in the kitchen. Annie ran to greet her and hugged her. Ruth came up shyly and slipped an arm around Meghan's waist, resting her head briefly against her side.

Meghan felt her own heart spill over with joy.

"Meghan. Look what Uncle Luke gave me. It belonged to my dad." Ruth picked up a crudely carved elk from the table with reverent hands. "Isn't it wonderful?"

"Wonderful," Meghan murmured, but her eyes were on Luke.

"Your dad did that when he was just about your age," he said. "I found it in the attic and figured you might like to have it."

Ruth fingered the small carving. "Daddy made it?" At Luke's nod, she threw her arms around him. "Thanks, Uncle Luke. I love it. I'm going to put it in my room right now." She planted a noisy kiss on his cheek before running off.

Meghan felt her own eyes fill with tears. He'd gone searching for something of her father's to give to his niece, something to ease the strain of what could have been a painful day . . . and she fell in love all over again.

Luke looked up at her, pulled a handkerchief from his pocket, and handed it to her. "Here. You look like you could use this."

She accepted it gratefully and dabbed at her eyes. "Thanks. That was a beautiful thing you did."

An embarrassed flush deepened the color in his tanned face. "It was just lying around. I thought Ruth might like it."

She wasn't fooled. The man had taken the time to help his niece through a difficult time. He would hate it if he knew she'd elevated him to hero status, but for a minute she couldn't help it. Some of what she felt must have shown in her eyes.

"Don't go making me into some kind of hero," he warned. "It was only right that Ruth should have it."

Meghan flattened her palm against his cheek. "You can keep your tough-guy image. But I know better."

He looked so uncomfortable that she wanted to laugh. He worked so hard to hide what was so clear to her. Whether he admitted it or not, he was a hero . . . in her eyes.

"You're a good man, Luke MacAllister."

He tumbled her down into his lap. "We're good together."

She couldn't deny it. She snuggled closer and traced a finger along his jaw. Slightly stubbled, it felt rough, but she didn't mind. The texture was a pleasant one, a contrast with her own softer skin. She curved her lips over his, her arms sliding comfortably around his waist.

She loved this man with all her being. How long would it take before he could accept his own feelings?

An invitation from Luke to spend the day riding was too good to resist. The day was a gift, one she didn't intend to waste.

Mountains laced with snow towered in the distance. She smiled, remembering her first impression of them—whipped cream–topped sundaes. Night was coming sooner now, bringing a chill to the air and causing her to huddle inside her jacket.

She didn't regret the coming of winter. It was a time to settle in, to take stock of herself and her life. She knew enough to understand that winter brought its own set of problems to the ranchers. To Luke.

He wasn't some gentleman rancher, content to sit at home while others worked his land. She'd seen for herself that he worked harder than anyone on his payroll.

She didn't fully understand this land, not yet, but she could feel herself falling in love with it. Strange. She'd never felt this way about Seattle, where she'd spent most of her life. There, she'd felt like a passerby, shown only the tourist sights. She'd been insulated from real life by her father's money, his position, his ideas of what was proper for his daughter to witness.

Luke gave her a foot up, adjusted the stirrups, and pronounced her ready.

The little paint had a surefooted gait. Her confidence grew as she adapted to the rocking-horse feel of riding. She freed her hair from its clip and let the wind have its way.

He rode with an easy grace, one she could only envy. A companionable silence settled between them. She sensed they were sharing more than a ride. By inviting her to go riding with him, Luke was sharing a part of his life with her—a very important part.

Luke half turned in his saddle and gave her a thumbs-up sign. The small gesture bolstered her assurance, and she picked up her pace.

Brownie responded with a whinny, announcing

her pleasure at the faster gait. Meghan leaned over her neck and whispered, ''Let's catch up with him.''

Brownie didn't need a second urging. She took off with a bone-jarring gait. Meghan grabbed hold of the horn and held on. They passed a startled Luke, who took off after them. He caught the reins and pulled Brownie to a stop.

''Showing off?'' he asked after he'd made sure she was all right.

She drew a shaky breath. ''Never again.''

He dismounted, then came around to her side and helped her down, his hands warm on her waist. He took her hands in his and brought them to his lips.

She was dismayed to find her hands trembling beneath his mouth and felt her heart give a nervous jerk. Her breath stuck in her throat, and she sucked in a lungful of air.

''You know how I feel about you.'' He paused, and she prayed for the words she'd longed to hear. ''I love you.'' His voice was deeper than usual, his hands not quite steady as he fitted them around her waist. There, with the sunlight in her hair, turning it to the color of dark honey, he kissed her.

I love you. Three simple words, words that had the power to change lives. Her life.

''I'm hoping you feel the same,'' Luke said in that same husky voice.

''You know I do.''

''Juanita was right, you know,'' he said.

"She was?"

"She called you my heartsong."

"Heartsong?"

"That's what the Indians call it." He took her hand and placed it on his heart. "I carry you here. Whether we're together or apart."

The idea touched her, but not as much as the tenderness in his voice. "And you are mine."

He dropped to one knee and took her hand in his. "Meghan Sullivan, will you marry me?" He didn't give her time to answer as he went on in a rush of words, "I've got no right asking you, not when I've still got a mountain of debts to pay off."

"Did you mean what you said? That you love me?"

"You know I do."

"Then you have every right to ask me."

He stood, then cupped her shoulders, bringing her close enough that she could smell the clean male scent of him. "I want to be able to give you everything you deserve."

"You and Annie and Ruth are everything I want, everything I need."

His gaze settled on her with a warmth that belied the autumn chill. "I'll make you happy. I swear it."

"You already have."

His lips covered hers in a kiss so sweet and tender that tears filled her eyes. When he lifted his head and stared at her with those beautiful gray eyes, she knew a sweet fulfillment.

"We need to make plans," he said. "How do you feel about a Christmas wedding? We could do it right here at the ranch."

"I love Christmas weddings."

He chuckled. "How many have you been to?"

"This'll be the first." She could see it now. Ruth and Annie as flower girls in red velvet, herself in a long, white gown, carrying a bouquet of fresh greens and red roses. The picture, so vivid, took on details. Luke would be more handsome than ever in a dark suit and snowy shirt. They'd have the wedding at his house, make it a family affair with just a few close friends present. Following the ceremony, there'd be a party. They'd invite the whole town.

"I know it's probably not what you had in mind when you were engaged before," Luke said.

Her lips curved at the idea. No, it wasn't the society wedding she'd planned with Trent. Thank goodness. It would be a family one.

"I can't promise it'll be the fanciest wedding there ever was," Luke said. "But we'll do it up any way you want. The ladies in town will most likely want to help."

"All I want is you." She lifted his hand to her lips and pressed a kiss to his palm. "I'll do my best to make you happy. All of you."

"You already do," he said, echoing her words of a few moments ago.

"When we're married, I can help."

His lips kicked up at the corners. "You gonna learn how to run the tractor?"

She poked him in the arm. "I mean really help. I've got some ideas . . . I've been reading up." Shy now, she gestured toward the fields, dark and fallow in the distance. "I wondered about sowing natural grasses in the spring."

He appeared to think about it.

"There's got to be a reason for what grows native here."

"You've got a point there."

Encouraged, she said what else was on her mind. She took a breath. Then another. "What you said about paying off the debts . . . I have some money."

That earned a tired smile from him. "Meghan, I appreciate the offer. But I couldn't take your money. Besides, it would take a fortune to pay off what I owe."

"I have a fortune." She said the words quietly.

His smile grew a bit. "A fortune? On a teacher's salary?"

"My grandmother left me some stock."

"A few shares of stock—"

"It's more than a few shares." She drew a long breath and let it out. "I have a hundred thousand shares of Tycon Electric." Everyone knew of Tycon, an upstart company that ten years ago had moved into the big leagues. Her grandmother had invested in the business when it had been operating out of the owner's garage.

"A hundred thousand shares?" He spaced the words out, as though trying to make sense of them. "Why didn't you say anything before now?"

"It didn't seem important. I knew it wouldn't make any difference to you." A nervous laugh rattled from her. She didn't understand why, but she knew she'd crossed some kind of line, something that was important.

He was silent for a long time. Too long. She choked down the knot that had formed in her throat and forced herself to wait.

"How do you know that?" he asked at last.

"Because I know *you.* You would never marry a woman for money. The only reason you'd ever marry is for love." She said the words with absolute conviction. How could he think she would doubt him or his motives? Luke was the most honest man she knew.

"If this gets out, people'll think I married you for your money."

She couldn't believe he was serious. "No one who knows you would believe that."

"People get funny ideas when it comes to money. Especially the kind of money you're talking about."

"So what if they do? We know better."

"Do you?"

The change in pronoun wasn't lost on her. *We* had become *you*. How had that happened? Only moments ago they were talking about a future . . . a future together. Now there was only him and her, no *us*.

He took a step back. It did more than put space between them. It defined the distance separating them. A distance she felt growing with every passing moment.

She wasn't naive enough to believe it would all be smooth sailing, but she didn't expect obstacles to appear so quickly. Especially one about her inheritance. If she'd known, she'd have kept it to herself. Slowly, she shook her head. Luke needed to accept her as she was.

"I know why you love me," she said, choosing her words carefully. "And it has nothing to do with how much money I have. If I had nothing, would that stop you from marrying me?"

"Of course not." He looked so offended that she wanted to laugh. She would have, if the situation had been different, if her heart hadn't been breaking. "Then why does it matter that I have some stock?"

"A hundred thousand shares isn't *some*. It's a fortune. A fortune." The last came as the barest whisper, as though it hurt him to say the words.

She was hurting too. "So it *is* a question of

money. You don't want me because I have too much."

Put that way, it sounded ridiculous. He didn't intend arguing with her. "If we get married, it's my job . . . my privilege . . . to take care of you."

"If?" One small word that could changes lives. "Does that mean you don't want to marry me anymore?"

She was turning him inside out, making him say things he didn't mean. "Of course not," he said again. But the words lacked confidence. He heard the uncertainty that lay beneath them. From the look on her face, Meghan had too.

She was blinking back tears, tears he'd put there.

He started toward her, only to have her back away. He'd try another tack. "Look around you."

He'd focused his efforts on rebuilding the fences and corrals, reasoning that cosmetic improvements could wait. But looking at it through Meghan's eyes, he saw the peeling paint and splintered wood of the house. Sunlight glinted off the tin roof of the barn, dimpled by a hailstorm.

The gardens, once a showplace, now bore the bedraggled look of the rest of the place.

Slowly, he was rebuilding the ranch into what it had once been, but it took time. Too much time. And bone-breaking work. He said as much.

She let her gaze follow his before she brought it back to settle on him, her eyes narrowing. "Do you think I'm so weak-kneed that I can't handle a little work?'' She held out her hands. ''Look. See these? They're blisters. I earned them. Digging up a garden.''

He resisted the urge to squirm under the derision in her voice. ''It's a heck of a lot more than a little work.'' He caught her chin in his hand and forced her to look at the neglected state of the house, the barn that could use a new coat of paint, the shabby outbuildings.

''You're right,'' she said, her gaze settling on him. ''I don't like what I see.''

The satisfaction he should have felt at her words was conspicuously absent. ''You're finally seeing what a dump this place is.''

''What I'm finally seeing is you. You're a snob, Luke.''

His head jerked up at that. He looked as angry as one of the wild stallions he tried to tame.

She felt a flare of hope unfurl inside of her. If she could stir that kind of anger within him, he must feel something for her. Anger didn't exist without feeling. Just as quickly, the anger faded, and he looked at her with eyes so blank that she felt chilled.

Her brief stir of hope faltered and died.

She couldn't resist touching him once more. She laid her hand against his cheek and held it there. A muscle twitched in his jaw. Abruptly, he turned away from her.

Grateful his back was to her, she squeezed her eyes shut and bit down on her lip to keep from bawling like a baby. She got herself under control before he turned around to face her. "Good-bye, Luke. If you decide you can accept me as I am . . ." She broke off, hoping the small shrug hid the sob she felt rising in her throat. ". . . you know where to find me."

It took everything she had to turn and walk away. Everything and more. *Please*, she prayed silently, *don't let him follow*. She couldn't bear his anger. Or worse, far worse, his pity. Her knees were shaking so badly by the time she reached her car, she could barely open the door.

She managed to collapse on the seat before the pain started. Great waves of it washed over her. She gasped in gulps of air in an effort to steady herself. Several minutes passed before she could trust herself to turn on the ignition and pull out of the drive.

She was grateful for the settling dusk. The trip home required all her concentration. Pulling to a haphazard stop in her driveway, she turned off the key. Her hands still gripping the steering wheel, she stayed where she was, unable to move.

Seconds bled into minutes and still she sat. When she started to the house, her legs felt leaden. Once inside, she leaned against the closed door and shuddered. The trembling started in her legs and eventually claimed all of her. When, at last, her legs didn't threaten to buckle, she stumbled into her bedroom. She didn't bother to turn on the lights. Darkness suited her mood.

Everything she'd ever wanted could have been hers. It had been close enough that she'd believed it within her reach. So close, but not close enough, she thought. Not close enough.

In the window frame, a small spider was carefully spinning a gossamer-fine web. She watched his patient efforts, thinking of her own attempt to build a new life.

She'd come here to heal, but more than that, to start over, to put the past behind her and find the strength to begin again. Instead, she felt more vulnerable, more lost than ever. Despite her brave words to her father, she felt as fragile, as easily broken as that newly spun web.

The web grew almost imperceptibly. Despite its delicate appearance, it was strong. And so was she, she promised herself. She'd survived losses before. She would again.

A small voice reminded her that no loss could equal that of Luke. She held on to the hope that he'd understand that accepting her help didn't make him any less of a man. She remembered his tenderness, his unconditional love for Ruth and Annie. The tears started again. This time she let them have their way.

* * *

Luke watched as Meghan drove away. Pain, unexpected and sharp, slammed into his gut. Automatically, he flattened a hand against his stomach. But nothing could ease the growing pressure there, or the sense of loss.

His body craved action, demanded he go after her, make her listen. Instinct told him to give her time.

Meghan didn't understand. A man took care of his woman, his children. He didn't lean on anyone, especially those he'd sworn to protect. A sigh leaked out of his lungs.

He wanted to provide for Meghan, just as he did Annie and Ruth. Why couldn't she understand that? Taking her money just wasn't acceptable.

She'd come around, he told himself. As soon as she realized that he was right, she'd be back.

He wondered why he didn't feel any better.

When Meghan didn't show up the next day or the day after that, Luke started to worry. He started to go to her when he thought better of it. Maybe it was for the best.

How long would she be content here? How long before she grew bored with what ranch life could offer? What *he* could offer?

He couldn't give her a fancy house with servants to wait on her. Or designer clothes. Or anything a woman like her was accustomed to.

Sure, she might think the idea of playing rancher's wife sounded fun. But what about when the temperature dropped to ten below zero and the calves had to be fed? How would she feel when he was gone from sunup to midnight and came home so bone-tired that he could barely stand, much less take her out dancing? And what of the crueler parts of ranching—the branding, the castrating, the putting down of animals too sick to save?

How could he expect Meghan to cope with that kind of life? A lot of women born and bred to it couldn't handle the hardships. He'd seen it more than once. His own mother hadn't been able to bear the isolation, the back-breaking work, the bitter cold of winter, the sun-baked dryness of summer.

He had to be fair to Meghan, no matter what the cost to him. And what about Annie and Ruth? They already loved her. What would it do to them to make her a part of the family and then have her leave?

His lack of honesty shamed him. It wasn't Annie and Ruth he was looking out for. It was himself. To have Meghan look at him one day as nothing more than a promise she must keep would destroy him. He knew that as surely as he knew his own name. He couldn't chance it. Better a half life without her, than to risk losing his soul when she left him.

The questions swarmed around inside his mind, tormenting, taunting, until he could no longer think.

He snapped at Ruth when she asked him to help her with long division. He cut Juanita off when she asked what he'd like for dinner. He nearly bit off

George's head in an argument about where to winter the main herd.

After dinner, which no one had even pretended to eat, he stomped outside, needing solitude. Without bothering to think where he was going, he headed to the truck, turned on the ignition, and drove as though demons pursued him.

He started cross-country, not bothering to stick to the roads. This was the land of his childhood. He knew every mountain, every valley and ridge. His truck took the rough ground with scarcely a hitch. How long he drove, he couldn't have said. When he found himself at the edge of a canyon, staring down at the emptiness below, he stopped. Stared.

The place was as cold and empty as the black hole of his heart.

Chapter Eight

A cold snap had hit the state. A fire, Luke decided, would take away the chill. Expertly, he laid the logs, struck a match, and watched it catch hold. It hissed a bit, sputtering and spitting. Smoke huffed once, twice, stirred by the wind.

Flames crackled, a familiar sound that should have soothed and comforted. Not tonight. The warmth settled over him, but it failed to erase the chill in his heart. When a knock sounded at the door, he raised his head and barked, "What?"

Juanita pushed open the door, carried a tray across the room, and set it on his desk. "Eat."

"I'm not hungry."

She planted her hands on her hips and scowled at him.

He scowled back.

144

She waited.

Knowing she had the tenacity of a bulldog and wouldn't budge until he'd at least tasted the food, he took a bite of the stew. It was good. The rumbling of his stomach reminded him that he hadn't had anything to eat since breakfast. Truth was, his appetite had been off for the last week.

Grudgingly, he finished the stew, sopping up the last bit of gravy with a roll. He pushed the plate away and glared up at her. "Satisfied?"

"No."

He didn't bother asking what else she wanted. Juanita wasn't one to be rushed. She'd tell him in her own way, her own time.

Apparently, that time was now. "You've been acting like a bear with its head caught in a beehive." She used the same tone she'd used when Luke was ten and throwing a tantrum when his father wouldn't let him ride a new stallion.

He winced. "Thanks for the observation. Anything else you wanted to say?"

"What I want doesn't matter. It's what you want."

To be left alone. No, that wasn't right. He wanted Meghan, but he couldn't have her.

"You want the schoolteacher," Juanita said when he remained stubbornly silent. "So you send her away. Not smart."

Trust Juanita to cut to the heart of the matter,

Luke thought. No mincing words for her. He considered firing her, and rejected it. He'd fired her at least a dozen times over the years, and each time, she'd ignored him. He was honest enough to admit that he couldn't manage without her. He was pigheaded enough to want to try.

"Why don't you mind your own business?" he asked, but the words were said without heat.

"You are my business," she said simply. "You and the little ones."

"It wouldn't have worked," he said at last. "Me and Meghan."

"She loves you."

"She doesn't belong here." *If he said the words often enough, he might begin to believe them.*

"Pride is a foolish man's burden. A lonely man's companion."

Luke pretended not to have heard.

"She is your heartsong," Juanita said quietly. "I know that, and so do you. Your father didn't raise a fool for a son, so why do you act like one?"

Her words continued to echo in his mind long after she left the room.

He stared at the fire, watched a log burn and then fall apart. Like his life, he thought sourly. Falling apart.

Luke scowled at the broken fence the following afternoon. Darn elk knocked the fences down faster than he and his men could repair them. Just what he needed.

The coming of winter didn't stop the operations of the ranch. If anything, the cold demanded more hours, more sweat, more worry. Grateful for the extra work, Luke rode fences, checked on the harvest, worried over the profit-and-loss statements at night.

Pretty soon he'd be deciding on what cattle would be wintered here, what would be shipped to feed pens for finishing. Then there was next year's planning and figuring. There were a dozen factors to take into consideration—birth and wean weights, pasture rotation, whether this was the year to implement his idea of breeding quarter horses.

He crammed more and more into each day, determined to crowd out thoughts of Meghan. He kept a tight hold on the reins of running the ranch, taking over what had once belonged to George and Tucker.

It was only a matter of time before one or both of them called him on it. That Tucker chose today, when Luke's temper was already on a short fuse, was just plain bad luck.

''Boss?''

Luke looked up from the fence post he was resetting to see Tucker shuffling from foot to foot. Just what he needed, he thought, as if things weren't bad enough already. ''Yeah?''

Tucker tugged at his kerchief as if it was suddenly

too tight around his neck. "Me and George...
we've been talking."

Luke waited, certain he wasn't going to like what
was coming.

"We...uh...think you ought to get back together with the pretty schoolteacher."

He was right. "You do, do you?"

Tucker cleared his throat. "Yeah. We do." He
made a gurgling sound and then spat out a wad of
tobacco. "You've been downright ornery ever since
you and her broke up."

"How do you know so much about my private
life?"

"Heck, Boss. Ain't nothing private around here."

How could he, Luke wondered, forget that in
Flintrock everyone knew everyone else's business
practically before they knew it themselves?

"She smells awfully sweet," Tucker said diffi-
dently. "A man could forget a lot of things with a
woman who smelled like that."

His fists curled at his sides, Luke reminded himself that there was no law against noticing how a
woman smelled. "You got a point to make?"

"I'm gettin' to it."

Luke bit back a sigh, knowing there was no use
in rushing him.

Tucker stuck his hands in his pockets. "If a
woman ever looked at me the way Miz Sullivan

looks at you, I'd fall down on my knees and promise her I'd love her forever.

''Well, I said what I came to say. I'd best be seeing to that . . . uh . . . that . . .'' He nearly tripped over his tongue.

Taking pity on him, Luke said, ''Yeah. You'd better.'' He watched his friend take himself off and turned back to work.

But his mind wasn't on repairing fences. It was remembering the scent that was Meghan's alone, the feel of her as she wrapped her arms around him, the softness of her mouth when he feathered his lips over hers.

What had made him think he was getting over her? He was as much in love with her as ever. He jammed the hole-digger into the ground and tried to obliterate the picture of Meghan's face that had stuck in his mind.

His efforts were wasted, as he'd known they would be.

He studied the sky, the white, fluffy clouds that clung to the mountain peaks. They looked like pretty cotton puffs, but he didn't trust them. If a person looked closely, he'd see the underlying layer of gray, a gray that hinted at rain.

Heaven knew they needed the moisture. But it wasn't likely to be a gentle patter that the earth could absorb at its own rate. No, more probably, it would be a hard-hitting rain which would batter and pummel the ground, making flooding a danger.

At one time, the uncharacteristic pessimism wouldn't have worried him. It wasn't his nature to look on the dark side. Lately, though, that's all he'd been able to see.

His sense of doom thickened. For what seemed the thousandth time, he told himself it was for the best—his breakup with Meghan. A woman like Meghan would soon grow bored in a hole-in-the-wall like Flintrock. He had nothing to offer but a truckload of debts and a ready-made family.

He knew she said she didn't mind the isolation, the lack of money, the unending work. But what about six months from now, a year or two? And what of Ruth and Annie? Meghan cared for them. There was no denying that. But how did she feel about taking on another woman's children as her own . . . on a permanent basis?

Ranching was a twenty-four-hour-a-day, three-hundred-sixty-five-day-a-year job. There were no paid vacations, benefits packages, or any other perks except the satisfaction a man found from looking out upon his own land.

He lifted his head and saw it now—the corrals, the outbuildings, the paddocks, and farther to where the land rolled forth to meet the sky. The endless expanse of land and sky was balm to his wounded spirits.

MacAllisters had worked the land for well over a hundred years—his pa, his pa before him, the one before him. It was as much a part of him as was the Indian blood that ran through his veins. Caring for it was his heritage. And his charge.

A wry smile twisted his mouth as he thought about what he had to offer: impossible hours, bitter cold in the winters, too-short summers, and work enough to break a man if he let it. Not much to recommend it, nothing except that it was all he'd ever known, all he'd ever wanted.

What kind of woman would want to share it? The job of a rancher's wife was no less demanding. Feeding twenty hands during roundup, tending the minor cuts and injuries that came with ranch life, pulling calves in the middle of the night, living with a husband too tired to do more than pull off his boots and fall into bed at night. Yeah, it was a picnic, all right. A real picnic.

It was his life, though, and he loved it with a passion as big as the land itself.

The arguments fell flat as he acknowledged that life without Meghan was no life at all.

Meghan scowled out the school window at the darkening sky. The grayness that stared back at her gave shape to the sadness that had colored her mood.

''Meghan?'' Annie MacAllister tugged at Meghan's skirt. ''Can we talk?''

"Sure." Meghan felt a smile bloom on her face. It felt right there, good after the pain of the last few weeks. The rest of the children had left for the day. Only Annie and Ruth remained. Ruth was busy with the new computer.

She took Annie's hand, pulled the little girl to her, and hugged her tightly.

"I miss you," Annie said, wriggling out of the embrace.

Meghan blinked back the tears that fell all too easily these days. "I miss you too." Her voice cracked on the last word. Or was it her heart?

"Why don't you come and see us anymore?"

"I . . . uh . . . I've been really busy." The reproach in Annie's eyes shamed Meghan into adding, "I thought it might be best if I didn't come over so much anymore."

"Because you're mad at Uncle Luke." Annie nodded wisely. "Why are you mad at him?"

Meghan looked at Annie and felt her heart break a little more. "I'm not mad at your uncle," she said slowly.

"Are you mad at Ruth and me?"

"Oh, no," Meghan cried, cuddling Annie close to her despite the little girl's wiggling. "Why would you think that?"

This time, Annie seemed content to stay in her arms. "You said you weren't mad at Uncle Luke.

And you don't come around anymore. So you must be mad at me or Ruth.''

"Your uncle and I had a misunderstanding. That's why I don't come around anymore. It has nothing to do with you and Ruth. We'll always be friends.''

"Best friends?'' Annie asked, her eyes solemn.

"Best friends,'' Meghan promised.

"But come the end of the year, you'll go away.'' Annie's chin wobbled.

There was no way to argue with that and come out on the right side of the truth. Annie deserved better from her. And she would miss her and Ruth, she added to herself. Ruth and Annie had made a place for themselves in her heart.

She didn't want to say good-bye. She rested her cheek on top of Annie's head and drew a shaky breath, inhaling Annie's warm little-girl smell mixed with the dirt she'd managed to collect at recess. The action felt so familiar, so *right*. Meghan didn't think she'd ever forget the sensation of holding Annie and Ruth in her arms.

The comfort she received reminded her of something else, something decidedly less comfortable. Luke. The scent of hardworking male that she'd become so aware of during the last months.

Annie squirmed in her arms, drawing Meghan's thoughts back to the here and now.

"How 'bout you and Ruth and I go collecting leaves after school tomorrow?'' Meghan suggested.

The idea took shape in her mind. The trees were heavy with leaves just beginning to fall. She pictured the girls scampering in the brightly colored leaves.

"Just the three of us? What about Uncle Luke?"

"I'm sure your uncle's very busy right now, too busy for leaf-collecting."

Annie's shoulders slumped. "He's busy all the time." Her tone, more than the words themselves, told Meghan how hurt she was feeling, how lonely.

She knew a surge of anger toward Luke. Just because he'd chosen to be pigheaded about their relationship was no reason to cut off the girls as well. Anger died, to be supplanted by regret. Luke loved his nieces. She knew that, had never doubted it. If he were distant now, it was because he was hurting.

"I wish you could stay forever, Meghan." Annie's innocent words cut through Meghan's musings.

"Forever is a long time," Meghan said lightly. She brushed a kiss across Annie's forehead. "I'd love to stay forever. But sometimes things don't work out the way we want them to."

Already there was talk of bussing the children to a county school next semester. Some members of the town council weren't satisfied with the way things were going. The family-type school she'd come to love would die in the name of progress.

Now wasn't the time to go into that. Not with Annie looking at her with such trust, such love.

"If you go away, I'll never see you again," Annie said, looking as if she were about to cry.

"Hey, we're friends, aren't we? Friends stay friends. No matter where they live or how far apart they are." Meghan hugged the little girl to her and squeezed tightly. "I love you. Nothing's going to change that."

Annie seemed to accept that, and Meghan drew a sigh of relief. They started to make plans for tomorrow's outing. Annie's enthusiasm was contagious, and Meghan found herself responding to it.

"Annie, come on," Ruth called. "Juanita's here."

Juanita still came every afternoon to pick the girls up. Meghan had taken to avoiding the housekeeper, knowing that she saw too much. How could she explain to Juanita that she and Luke didn't have what it took to see them through the first day of their engagement, much less a lifetime together?

Instead, she gave Juanita a distant smile as she saw the girls off, breathing a sigh of relief when the older woman didn't try to talk with her.

Coward, she berated herself.

Dinner at Belle's might take her mind off her troubles, Meghan decided. The now familiar aroma of cinnamon rolls took the edge off the day, and she inhaled deeply. After giving her order of meat loaf with all the fixings, she sank back in the booth and let the mingled sounds of conversation and jukebox music wash over her.

It was just her bad luck that tonight was the monthly meeting of the Flintrock school board. To add insult to injury, the waitress seated the members at the booth across from Meghan's. The only thing that saved her was Luke's absence. Whatever fates had conspired to cause him to miss the meeting, she silently thanked them.

She pretended to study the place mat covered with knock-knock jokes and bad puns. She told herself it didn't bother her that conversation stopped when Hattie and the others noticed her. She congratulated herself that she didn't mind the quickly averted gazes and hushed voices, the awkward smiles and even more awkward greetings.

Sure, she didn't.

Her food arrived. She looked at it and wondered what had made her order meat loaf in the first place. Swimming in gravy, it nearly made her gag. When she'd spent a respectable amount of time pushing the food around on her plate, she slapped some money on the table and slid out of the booth.

And pretended not to hear Hattie's voice calling to her as she made her way out of the diner.

Barbed wire.

He hated the stuff. Years of working with it hadn't changed that. If he hadn't spent so much time mooning over Meghan, he'd have finished the job yesterday.

Luke muttered something under his breath as he tried to set a staple in the fence post. He tipped his hat back and scanned the sky. The weather wasn't any better than his mood. Clouds, pregnant with rain, loomed overhead. As if to confirm his suspicion, a spattering of raindrops splashed in his face, and he shook his head to clear the water out of his eyes. He hit the staple off center. It flew out of his wet fingers. The coiled wire he'd been trying to tighten slipped free and lashed out at him.

Snapping his head back, he managed to avoid the worst of it, but not before one of the barbs caught him across the jaw. He swiped at his face with the back of his hand, not surprised when his glove came away bloody.

Well, he couldn't spare the time to take care of it now. If he didn't get this fence mended before the rain really started, he'd have to wait until the ground dried out. Fencing and mud didn't mix.

Just a couple more to go. Resolutely, he picked up the wire and finished the post before moving on to the next one. By the time he finished, the rain had picked up, and he decided to call it a day. He headed to the pickup, stowed his gear in the back, and prayed the ancient truck would start. It tended to act up when it got wet.

The engine sputtered to life, and Luke breathed a silent prayer of relief.

The last thing he needed was to be stuck in the far pasture with no transportation. Tonight, he promised himself, he'd spend some time with the girls. He knew they were upset that Meghan didn't come around any more. He also knew they blamed him.

Living off his wife's money didn't sit well with him. Heck. He couldn't do it. He *wouldn't* do it. A man had his pride. The argument sounded hollow, even to his own ears. Pride was a lonely companion, as Juanita had reminded him.

Wet, cold, and hungry, he didn't have the energy or inclination to sort through his emotions. He wanted a hot shower, dry clothes, and a warm meal—in that order. Then he'd show the girls that they could still be a family. Even without Meghan.

He pulled in in front of the house. He sat there a moment, slumped behind the wheel, and tried not to think of her.

Of course, he thought of her.

He forced a smile to his face when he saw Ruth fly out of the front door. He got out of the truck and rounded it. "How's my best ten-year-old girl?" He took her hand and pulled it into the crook of his arm, closing his own hand over hers.

She yanked it away. "Nice of you to show up."

He heard the snap in her voice and winced. He supposed he deserved that. He hadn't been around much lately, purposefully distancing himself. Skipping last night's school-board meeting to spend time with the girls hadn't improved his stock much, not when both of them had stared at him with accusing eyes and demanded to know when Meghan was coming back. "What is it, honey?"

"It's Annie."

"What about her?"

"We can't find her. Anywhere."

He wasn't particularly worried. Annie often played hide-and-seek. She was probably in the barn, giggling to herself over the trick she'd played.

"Don't you get it? Annie's gone!" Ruth shouted the words through her tears and pounded on his chest. "Did you hear me? Or don't you care?"

He gathered her small fists in his hands and stilled them. "Are you sure?" He felt the first stirring of fear. Still, he didn't panic. Annie could be in any of a hundred different places. All they had to do was find the right one.

Ruth pulled away from him. "Of course I'm sure. You think I'm some stupid kid who'd make up a story like that?"

"No. No. Was she worried about something?"

"She was real sad about you and Meghan breaking up."

"I know she was upset, but—"

"She was more than upset. She wanted Meghan

to be our mom. We both did. Maybe if you were around more, you'd know.''

The sting of guilt cut deeply. He'd been well and truly put in his place by his niece.

''Did you tell Juanita?''

''Juanita told me to come and find you.''

''Tell Juanita I'm coming.'' He kept his voice calm. Of course they'd find Annie. It was simply a matter of looking in the right place.

A half hour later, he wasn't so sure. Annie wasn't in the house or the barn or any other of the outbuildings. For what seemed the hundredth time, Luke reminded himself not to panic.

She wasn't at any of her friends' houses. He cautioned himself not to give in to the fear rising in his throat.

''What about Meghan?'' Ruth asked. ''Annie's been talking about her a lot.''

Of course. If he hadn't been so caught up in guilt and fear, he would have thought of her earlier.

He rode to Meghan's, afraid to hope, afraid not to hope. Panic clawed at him, insidious and all-consuming.

He found her working in the small garden plot at the back of the house. He wondered what kind of welcome he'd find. There was no time for feeling awkward, not with Annie missing.

Meghan looked up, her face flushed, her hands

caked with dirt. "Luke." The pleasure in her eyes faded. "What's wrong?"

"Annie's missing."

"How long?"

She didn't waste time asking useless questions, Luke thought with a flash of appreciation. She got right to the point.

"Two hours."

"You've already searched the ranch, of course."

He nodded wearily. "And called her friends. I thought maybe she'd come here. She said something last night—"

"What?" she prompted.

"She misses you."

"Oh."

"Yeah." He swallowed. They both knew why Meghan hadn't been around to the ranch, why Annie missed her.

"I'll come with you." She turned toward the house.

"No." The word, sharp as a slap, stopped her in her tracks. "I mean, it'd help if you'd check the woods back of your house. George and Tucker and me, we'll spread out from the ranch and work our way back to you. She can't have gotten much farther than that." He prayed.

She spared a moment to skim her fingers down his jaw. "We'll find her, Luke."

In the dim light of dusk, his face was all rough

angles and shadowed planes, his eyes bleak and full of self-accusation. A single tear slid down his cheek. He was a strong man, a proud man. No one knew that better than she did. But pain and fear undid him. Her heart wept for him, but she knew enough not to offer sympathy.

He reached for her and then dropped his hand before touching her. "Thank you."

She wanted to touch him again too. That one brief contact wasn't enough. Not nearly enough. She, too, didn't follow through. "I'll be starting out as soon as I've changed."

"Meghan." She paused, turned. "Thanks."

Chapter Nine

The leaden sky promised rain. Normally, a rancher prayed for rain. Not now, though. Rain would turn the ground treacherous. The temperature was steadily dropping, another danger.

The wind slapped at him, all angry nails and claws. He staggered forward, only to be pushed back by its force. For every step he took, it seemed he lost two.

A small girl alone in the mountains. He tried to push the image from his mind, but it persisted. Everyone on the ranch, with the exception of Juanita, who had stayed with Ruth, was searching. He'd enlisted the help of the town as well. More than two dozen people were combing the woods, the fields, the foothills.

It might not be enough. The words pounded

through his mind, tormenting, taunting, torturing him with their implications. He knew the odds against finding one five-year-old girl.

He also knew he had no choice but to continue as he was. Railing against fate wouldn't change things.

The rain, which had threatened all day, started. No gentle patter, this. It came in great torrents. Lightning stabbed the sky, jagged slashes of fire.

Doggedly, he kept going. He wished he could see his way more clearly. There were only vague impressions of shapes and sizes, ominously dark, ominously large. How much darker, larger would they appear to Annie? He nearly tripped over an exposed root. Swearing softly, he caught himself before he plunged to the ground.

Cold, a furtive enemy, crept through his clothes, chilling him right down to the bone. He tugged his jacket closer around him and tried not to think of the thin shirt and jeans he knew Annie had been wearing.

A torn scrap of material had snagged on a branch, catching his attention. The rain had all but obliterated the colors, but he thought he could make out faint red checks.

Annie had been wearing a red shirt.

He scanned the gunmetal sky. The rain showed no indication of letting up.

Neither did he.

* * *

Crying.

Meghan halted her tromping through the woods and listened. She wasn't mistaken.

"Annie? Where are you?"

More crying. She could barely make it out above the roar of the wind and rain, but she caught it. Annie must be close.

Meghan followed the sound and realized it came from the river. Dread filled her at the implications. The rain had started in earnest, the water pouring down in great sheets that nearly blinded her. She knew enough to understand that the normally sluggish river would have swollen to twice, perhaps more, its normal size. She pushed on until she reached it.

Caution gave way to urgency, and she half ran, half slid down the steep bank, unmindful of the bushes that lashed her face and hands. The coppery taste of blood coated her mouth as a branch swung back to sting her lip. She swiped at her mouth with the back of her hand, smearing the blood. Shielding her eyes from the rain, she thought she saw a patch of red.

She squinted and made out a small figure.

Annie.

Meghan gave a whoop of joy. She'd found her. Her joy dissolved into confusion. Annie wasn't moving.

"I'm stuck," came the child's high-pitched cry.

Meghan swallowed tightly. The taste of fear—cold and bitter—was in her mouth. She recognized it immediately. Ruthlessly, she pushed it down. She couldn't afford the luxury of panic. Not now. Later, if . . . *when*, she corrected herself . . . when she freed Annie, she could give in to it.

Even from this distance, Annie looked pale. Too pale. How long had she been there? Meghan knew what prolonged exposure to the cold could do. Would do, if she didn't get Annie out of there and fast.

''I'm coming,'' she called.

She waded into the river and gasped. Cold such as she'd never felt before engulfed her. A dip in the river's bottom caused her to lose her footing and stumble. She caught herself before she went completely under. Drenched all the way to her shoulders, she shivered violently.

Meghan pushed her way forward until she was by Annie's side. She took the little girl's hands in her own and chafed them.

''I was hopscotching across the rocks,'' Annie said between chattering teeth. ''I slipped. Uncle Luke's gonna be real mad.''

''Your uncle will be happy you're all right,'' Meghan said. ''Now let's get you out of here.'' Silently, she prayed she could make good on her words.

She found the source of the trouble. Annie had caught her foot between the rocks.

Her fingers made clumsy by the cold, Meghan worked to free the little girl.

"I've . . . almost . . . got . . . it." Gasps of breath punctuated each word as she pulled the rocks away from Annie's foot. When the last rock gave way, Meghan pulled Annie into her arms and held tight. Relieved, she felt the little girl's heartbeat strong and sure.

"I want to go home." Annie whimpered into Meghan's shirt.

"I know, sweetie. I know."

The darkness deepened around them. The once lazy river had turned vicious.

Meghan shielded her eyes from the torrent of water as she scanned the distance to the shore. The few yards separating them from safety stretched endlessly.

"Come on," she urged Annie. "Let's get out of here."

Annie clung to her, her slight weight feeling heavier with every moment as Meghan battled her way toward the riverbank.

Water, more precious than gold in times of drought, was their enemy now. She fought the current and knew she was losing. Her left arm around Annie's waist, Meghan scrabbled one-armed against the rapids. Cold leached the last bit of energy from her.

Boulders studded the riverbed. The current tossed her against a particularly sharp one. The blow stunned her, causing her to nearly pass out.

Sheer will kept her conscious. That and the fact that Annie's life depended upon her. She tightened her grip on the little girl. They would make it, she silently vowed. The alternative was unthinkable.

She tried to yell for help, but the wind screamed and howled, drowning out her voice.

''Hold on.'' The words, so faint that she was afraid she'd imagined them, sounded above the bellow of the wind.

''Hold on. I'm coming.''

The words came again. This time she knew she wasn't mistaken. Luke's voice, strong and urgent, reached her. Energy she didn't know she had surged through her. She spared a moment to look up, but couldn't see him through the downpour. Night had fallen like a black curtain.

Somehow, she managed to grab hold of a scraggly bush shooting up in the crevice between two boulders. Water buffeted her against the rocks. Again and again, her body took the blows, but she held on.

When she felt strong arms wrap around her, she didn't dare believe it.

''I've got you,'' Luke shouted above the roar of the water. ''I've got you both.''

She gave in to the luxury of leaning against his arm, relying on his strength.

''Can you hold onto her while I get us to shore?'' he yelled above the raging water.

Meghan managed a jerky nod.

With one arm around her waist, Luke towed them to the river's bank, his other arm pulling through the water, crablike. There, Tucker and George hauled them onto the ground.

Meghan lay on the muddy bank, unable to move, scarcely able to breathe. She heard Annie crying and tried to reach for her, but her legs and arms refused to obey her command.

''Annie . . .''

''She's all right.''

Gentle hands ran over her arms and legs, testing, probing. ''Nothing's broken as far as I can tell,'' she heard Luke say.

Shivers racked her body, even with the blankets George and Tucker had piled on top of her.

''We've gotta get her warm, boss,'' George said. ''She's going into shock.''

Luke felt her pulse. It was thready. He knew that hypothermia could set in within minutes, if it hadn't already.

He wrapped her and Annie in more blankets and hugged them to him.

''You're all right.'' The words were a prayer, a litany, a plea.

Within minutes, he and George and Tucker had erected a makeshift shelter out of a canvas tarp. Luke heated up some tea and managed to get some down both Meghan and Annie. When the color returned to their cheeks, he hoped they were out of danger. But they couldn't stay here.

"Let's get them home," he said shortly.

The trip home took twice as long as it ordinarily would have. Luke chafed with each minute that passed.

George carried Annie. Luke took Meghan. Tucker offered to spell him, but he refused. He needed to keep her near him. She faded in and out of consciousness. He tried not to think beyond putting one foot in front of the other. The ground, slippery from the rain, was as treacherous as the cold. He fought to keep his footing.

At the house, he rung up the doctor, who promised to be there within fifteen minutes. One of the benefits of living in a small town, he thought, was a doctor who made house calls.

After a brief exam, Doc Rimmer pronounced Annie all right. "Your friend's going to need a few days to recover," he said after checking out Meghan. "She's pretty banged up."

Luke nodded grimly. Meghan had taken a beating in the river. He knew she could have gotten herself to safety, but she'd stayed with Annie. He'd never forget what she'd done. Or forgive himself for letting her put herself in that kind of danger.

Luke saw the doctor off and then returned to sit by Meghan's side.

Annie shuffled into the room. "Uncle Luke, is Meghan gonna be all right?" The quiver in Annie's voice echoed Luke's own fears.

"She's gonna be fine, Pumpkin. Now you get back to bed. Okay?"

" 'Kay." She gave him a wet, sloppy kiss and scampered off.

He turned his attention back to Meghan. Her eyes flickered open.

"How're you feeling?" To his own ears, his voice sounded sandpaper-rough. He couldn't help it. The realization that she and Annie could have died in the river would take time to fade. Maybe a lifetime.

"All right."

He caught her chin in his hand and turned her face first one way, then the other. Satisfied, he nodded, and skimmed a hand across her cheek, as if to reassure himself that she was indeed all right. It wasn't enough. Gently, tenderly, he reached for her. At that moment, he could no more have stopped himself from taking her in his arms than he could have stopped breathing.

"What you did out there . . . I'll never be able to thank you enough."

She was still cold, but she didn't care. The warmth

in Luke's eyes was enough to heat her through and through. For a moment, she let herself hope that he'd learned to accept her—inheritance and all. Then she remembered. He was grateful for what she'd done for Annie. Things between them hadn't changed.

"If it hadn't been for you . . ." His voice broke, a ragged whisper that tore at her heart.

His face was gray, bleached almost to white in the dim light of the room. Anger tightened the lines around his mouth. She knew the target of that anger. Himself. Luke was a man to take on the blame even when it was no fault of his own.

"It's not your fault," she said quietly.

"You and Annie almost died. Whose fault do you think that is?"

"No one's. Nature's. But not yours. *Not yours.* And we didn't die. We're here and we're both all right." She chose her next words carefully, tamping down her urgency to make him see what she'd learned. "It's part of the cycle. You, me, Annie . . . we're all connected together."

Confusion shadowed his face, and she rushed to explain herself. "Sometimes we're lucky enough to save others. Sometimes they save us. That's the way life is. None of us can do all of the saving all of the time." Tentatively, she reached out to him.

He said nothing, but didn't pull away from her embrace. That gave her courage to continue.

"You saved my life today. If it hadn't been for

you, we'd never have made it out of the river," she pointed out.

"If it hadn't been for me, you and Annie would never have been there in the first place."

"How do you figure that?"

"I should have kept better watch on her. I knew she was fretting over . . . things."

Over you and me, Meghan translated, but she kept her thoughts to herself. Now wasn't the time to go into what had happened between Luke and herself.

"I work with kids all day, five days a week. Don't you think I know how easy it is to lose sight of one, even for a second? And that's all it takes. A second. A fraction of a second and one of them can disappear." She took his hands in hers. "It's over. We're all right." How many times would she need to say those words before he accepted them?

He wanted to believe her. She saw it in his face. "I went into the river after Annie because I wanted to. Because it was the right thing to do. Wouldn't you have done the same thing?"

She didn't expect an answer. Nor did she need one. Luke would always try to save those he loved. It was one of the reasons she loved him as she did. It was also a club he used to beat himself with when he failed.

"What happened today brought back a lot of old memories, didn't it? About Dan and his wife. The day they died."

''Yeah.''

''And some nightmares.'' She knew that she'd touched a nerve. She only prayed he could forgive her for raising the painful memories.

He went totally still. ''I was too late.'' He sounded weary right down to his soul.

''You couldn't have stopped what happened to them. You can't save everyone, Luke. Not even the people you love the most. Life doesn't work that way.''

''I was too late for Dan and Christine. I was almost too late for you and Annie.''

''*Almost*. You got there in time.''

''This time.'' When he turned away, she grabbed his arm, forcing him to look at her.

''Why are you so hard on yourself?'' she demanded, using the same words he'd tossed at her weeks ago.

''Old habits.''

''Give 'em up.'' She met his gaze fiercely. ''And stop blaming yourself.'' She held out her arm and pulled up her sleeve. ''These bruises will fade a lot faster than the guilt you insist on heaping upon yourself.''

He looked unconvinced.

''If you'd stop being so selfish, you'd see that I'm right.'' Impatience colored her voice.

''Selfish?''

"Believing that you can control everything that happens to people is a kind of selfishness."

"I don't—"

"Don't you?"

That stopped him. "Okay. So maybe I like to be in control."

She raised a brow. "Just maybe?"

A half smile touched his mouth. "Don't push it." He looked at her, a frown taking the place of the smile of a moment ago. "You're tired. You ought to be resting."

"I'll make you a deal. You promise to stop blaming yourself and I'll try to sleep."

"Deal."

The different layers of feeling this man generated in her took on a deeper texture. Respect, admiration, tenderness, and love, always love.

He brushed his lips across her forehead, much as he would Annie or Ruth, she thought with a trace of resentment. Tomorrow, she promised herself, she'd call him on it. Now, though, her body clamored for sleep. With barely a sigh, she closed her eyes.

Tendrils of golden hair escaped their band, haloing about her face and making her look like an angel, one who had taken a tumble on her way to earth.

Luke watched as she gave in to the sleep she so badly needed. He only wished he could slip into oblivion as easily. The acid of guilt ate away at his insides.

Meghan couldn't be right. He wasn't so egocentric as to believe he had to be in control of everything and everyone, was he? Only a fool thought he could control the world.

Yet hadn't he believed he was to blame for Dan and Christine's deaths?

He went to check on Annie. Curled next to Ruth, she looked little the worse for her ordeal. One small hand clutched Taffy. Luke tucked the blankets over his nieces and thanked heaven for the wonder of them. He kissed his fingers and pressed them against Annie's cheek, then Ruth's. Whatever else happened, he had the most precious gift of all in them.

The rain had dissolved into a weak trickle running through the gutters and down the drain. The night held a much-needed gentleness that had been denied to the day.

The mountains were a place where it seemed time had stopped, civilization but a distant memory. Wild and unfettered by the trappings man had brought to the wilderness, they beckoned to him.

He navigated the torturous road with practiced ease. When he reached a clearing, he stopped the truck and climbed out. The view stretched before him, a panorama of unmatched beauty.

Luke never came here without feeling transported back in time. That had always been the appeal for him, to escape to a time when none of his problems existed. The scenery, magnificent though it was, was secondary.

Still, he spared a glance for it. Mountains, stripped of their greenery, rose like altars to the sky. Gorges, deep and forbidding, scarred the land. In the distance, the river, his enemy just days ago, meandered peacefully through the valley.

The land worked its magic on him as it always did, pulling him into another dimension, teasing him to leave all his troubles behind. He gave himself up to the quiet and let the peace settle over him. When he'd absorbed the serenity of the mountains, he forced himself to examine the mess he'd made of his life.

He ticked them off one by one. The girls were barely speaking to him. His concentration was shot— he'd nearly lost an arm working the combine yesterday. And his men were giving him a wide berth.

All because of Meghan.

Meghan.

Against his wishes, she'd gone home the day following the accident. She'd told him he needed time alone with his nieces. She'd been right on target with that. The three of them had reached a new understanding, one he hoped to build on. If only he could find the same kind of peace with Meghan.

Nothing he had said to her made sense—to her, and scarcely to himself. Honesty forced him to admit he was running scared. He'd put up every available roadblock. When she'd calmly overridden them one by one, he'd taken off like a startled jackrabbit.

Meghan deserved better. He knew it. And he feared he couldn't give it to her. It had nothing to do with fancy cars and clothes and houses. He'd gotten past that, ashamed that he'd thought even for a moment those things could matter to a woman like Meghan.

The question was whether he deserved her, whether he dared take the chance to find out. Answers which had deluded him only days ago now seemed clear.

Meghan loved him. And he loved her. Together they could make something good.

In her, he'd found what had been missing in his own life. The love that comes from knowing another's heart as well as he knew his own. The love that keeps you going when all else has failed. The love that gives meaning to the quiet moments and passion to the others.

He only prayed he could find the words to tell her what was in his heart. All he had to do was convince her to give him a second chance. He started home.

Lately, he'd begun to think of *home* as wherever Meghan was. He wondered if she felt the same way. He hoped so.

The day beckoned, tempting her to leave behind the papers she was due to grade. Such a day deserved to be savored. Not bothering with a coat, she headed outside. The very air was a bath on the skin, the sun a warm caress.

She went to the meadow. Dew silvered the grass. The air was garden-fresh, peppery with the after-scent of the storm. Sunlight peeked through slits in the clouds, bright patches against the darker shadows.

She could smell the grass, still damp from the rain, and the earthy aroma of dirt. She inhaled deeply, savoring the scent of the recent rain. In the distance, she could make out the stream, now lazily meandering within its banks, the violence that had nearly cost Annie her life only a memory.

A shiver traced down Meghan's spine as she re-called those few moments where she feared the wa-ter would claim both their lives. If not for Luke, it undoubtedly would have. She pushed the frightening pictures away and concentrated on the beauty sur-rounding her. The scene stretched before her was enough to take her breath away. Mountains poked their peaks through low-slung clouds. The clouds themselves were cotton puffs against the bluer-than-blue sky. Sunshine filtered through them, dappling the ground in a crazy quilt of shadow and light.

A perfect day for a picnic. Memories rushed back of another such day, a picnic shared with a very special man. Memories were all she had now, and she hoarded them with the stinginess of a miser storing away his gold. The sun slipped lower in the sky and still she stayed.

Amethyst shadows dimpled the ground. Hints of the coming fall had put a tang in the air. Heat still clung to the day, but the evenings had cooled off. She shivered in her thin cotton shirt and hugged her arms to her. Goose bumps puckered her skin, but she scarcely noticed, as a sound overhead snagged her attention. She lifted her gaze. And gasped.

The white eagle. She held her breath, afraid to move, afraid she'd frighten it away.

The legend held that if you made a wish when you saw the white eagle, it would come true. Did she believe? Did she believe *enough*?

The bird, beautiful in the way only a wild thing can be, glided through the sky, its wingspan easily eight or nine feet. Pride and strength, she thought, a powerful combination. In an eagle. Or a man.

Luke had both in abundance. And so much more. If only he'd realize that he had so much more to offer than he realized. More than a mortgaged ranch. Even more than his family. If only . . .

Eyes closed, she wished for her heart's desire.

Luke took a deep breath. A warm, heavy feeling filled him. The feeling had a name. Forgiveness. Meghan had given him that. She'd taught him that his guilt was a kind of selfishness.

Believing that he could have prevented Dan and

Christine's deaths was a kind of vanity. He couldn't have kept them from speeding down the mountain any more than Meghan could have kept her mother from dying. All they could do was grieve and move on.

Now he was ready to let it go. And with that went the pain and bitterness. Anxious to share what he'd learned, he went to the cottage.

The emptiness he found there mocked his eagerness to find her. He stood by the truck, frowning, looking around. She'd done something here, he thought. Those roots she'd talked of were shallow yet, but they'd taken hold. The bulbs she'd planted wouldn't be showing until next spring, but the place had a feel to it that had been missing before. Curtains peeked from the window; potted flowers trimmed the porch. She'd turned it into a home.

When Meghan hadn't returned by dusk, Luke felt the first clutch of panic.

Where could she have gone? The school? He shook his head in answer to his question. A friend's house? That was a possibility, but one he rejected as he thought it through. Meghan wasn't the type to turn to others when she was hurting. She would work through it on her own. So where *would* she go?

The meadow.

He found her there. Relief made him weak.

She must have slept. Her eyes felt gritty, her neck stiff. She blinked, stared, blinked again.

Luke was there, hunkered down beside her.

She rubbed her eyes, certain she was dreaming. She reached out to frame his face with her palms. He looked, felt real.

"You're here?" The words came out as a question.

"I'm here."

Ribbons of wind whipped around her, causing her to shiver slightly. He pulled her against him, turning her back to him and wrapping his arms around her.

She felt safe. Warm. Loved. Still, she had to ask. "Why did you come?"

He remembered his frantic rush to see her, his impatience when he couldn't find her. It was more basic than that, though. And much more simple. "I needed you."

The words wrapped their way around her heart. "I saw the white eagle. I wished on it." She said the words shyly, not sure of his reaction. Needing to see his face, she turned in his arms. To her relief, he only smiled. "Why did you come?"

She'd wished on the white eagle? The knowledge warmed him. Would she ever stop surprising him? He hoped not.

"You are my heartsong," he said.

"And you are mine."

The eagle soared overhead, his cry a seal on the love they'd just declared.

Meghan turned in his arms. "It's your turn. Make a wish."

He settled his hands at her waist, drawing her to him. "I don't have to. It's already come true."

Chapter Epilogue

Six-year-old Annie tugged at Meghan's jeans.
"Can I hold him?"

"It's my turn," Ruth said.

"We'll all have plenty of chances to hold him,"
Meghan said.

She picked up month-old Lucas Daniel Mac-
Allister from his cradle and settled him into Annie's
waiting arms. The cradle, a MacAllister heirloom,
was fashioned out of rich, dark walnut, satiny
smooth to the touch. When Luke had told her that
both he and Dan had used the cradle, and their father
before them, she'd fallen in love with it. The nicks
and scratches along the rockers only added to its
appeal.

Lucas let out a lusty wail.

"Uncle Luke," Annie said, handing the squalling baby back to Meghan, "Lucas needs the lullaby."

Meghan settled the baby at her breast, smiling when his cries subsided to contented sucking.

Luke, freshly showered, slanted a grin at Meghan and swung both girls up in his arms. He planted a kiss on their cheeks before setting them down to pick up his guitar.

Don't you fret,
Little son of mine,
I've got a yarn to spin,
A story so fine.

"Sing the second verse," Ruth said.

So quit your crying,
No need to wail,
Come listen to this
Old cowboy's tale.

Meghan placed Lucas on her shoulder, patted his back, and was rewarded by a loud burp. Luke's gaze, full of love and tenderness, caressed her.

The wish she'd made on the white eagle had come true.